FIGHT THE FUTURE

OTHER *X-FILES* TITLES PUBLISHED BY HARPERPRISM

NOVELS

Goblins

Whirlwind

Ground Zero

Ruins

Antibodies

*Skin**

Goblins/Whirlwind (two in one)

NONFICTION

The Making of The X-Files

The Truth Is Out There:
The Official Guide to The X-Files, *Volume One*

Trust No One: The Official Guide to
The X-Files, *Volume Two*

I Want to Believe: The Official Guide to
The X-Files, *Volume Three*

The X-Files *Book of the Unexplained, Volume One*

The X-Files *Book of the Unexplained, Volume Two*

The Official Map of The X-Files

The X-Files *Postcard Book: Conspiracies*

The X-Files *Postcard Book: Monsters and Mutants*

The X-Files *Postcard Book: Unexplained Phenomena*

*coming soon

THE X FILES ™

FIGHT THE FUTURE

CHRIS CARTER

ADAPTED BY

ELIZABETH HAND

HarperPrism

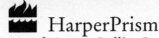
HarperPrism
A Division of HarperCollins*Publishers*
10 East 53rd Street, New York, NY 10022-5299

ISBN 0-06-105067-9

HarperCollins®, 📖®, and HarperPrism®
are trademarks of HarperCollins Publishers, Inc.

HarperPrism books may be purchased for educational, business,
or sales promotional use. For information, please write:
Special Markets Department, HarperCollins Publishers, Inc.
10 East 53rd Street, New York, NY 10022-5299.

Cover design © 1998 by Hamagami/Carroll & Associates
Cover artwork courtesy of and © 1998
Twentieth Century Fox Film Corporation.

First printing: July 1998

Designed by Lisa Pifher

Printed in the United States of America

Library of Congress Cataloging-in-Publication Data
is available from the publisher.

Visit HarperPrism on the World Wide Web at
http://www.harperprism.com

98 99 00 01 ❖ 10 9 8 7 6 5 4 3 2 1

FIGHT THE FUTURE

PROLOGUE

NORTH TEXAS
35000 B.C.

The desolated landscape stretches from horizon to horizon, all snow and ice and vast gray sky. In the distance two tiny figures appear, running desperately. They are manlike, with matted hair and coarse features, their bodies hidden beneath rough garments made of leather. They run across the white wasteland, bodies bent as if they are scanning the ground underfoot for prints. The trail they seem to follow leads to a crevice, a triangular fissure between slabs of ice and collapsed stone. At the mouth of the cave the prints disappear. One of the primitive men stoops to peer inside. They enter the cave.

Inside, the cave walls spiral; they are ribbed with ice that glistens faintly. The first primitive lights his torch. As he holds it up, his companion grabs his arm and points to where the cave twists a few yards ahead of them. There a soft patch of virgin snow bears the imprint of what they have been following. The torch sputters, and as though in reply a distinct scrabbling echoes back to them from the darkness ahead. The two primitives move quickly now. Ahead the cave splits into two tunnels. Wordlessly, they each choose a different fork.

The first primitive moves quietly through the tunnel. At the far end he finds an opening barely wide enough for a man to squeeze through. He thrusts his torch into the opening, twisting it back and forth. He propels himself through the hole and drops into the next chamber.

It takes a moment to catch his breath. When he does, he raises the torch and peers around. He is in a roughly circular cavern perhaps thirty feet across, its walls shimmering ice nicked here and there by rocky outcroppings. One of these is larger than the rest. Gazing at it, the primitive frowns, then steps toward it.

Inches away from the outcropping he halts and reaches to touch what he sees—the body of another man, clad in furs and leather, a skin of ice encasing him from head to foot. Before he can reach it something powerful strikes him from behind.

With a cry the primitive falls, the torch hurling from him to drop sputtering to the floor. He curls into a ball, one hand clenched against his chest with the knife pointing outward; but something is already there, claws tearing at his clothes, shredding the thick protective layers of fur and stiff leather as though they were dry grass. The primitive cries out again. He rolls to one side, shoving his elbow into the creature's face, and strikes blindly and desperately with his knife. It shrieks; he feels something warm and viscous spurt onto his hand. With a groan the primitive pulls away, staggering to the wall. He hears it thrashing in the darkness at his feet.

The primitive roars and strikes at it again, feels his knife shear through its skin. But there is no reassuring bite of bone and muscle beneath his hand; it is as though his knife is mired in the body. With a grunt the primitive yanks his knife back.

Too fast. The next instant he loses his balance and falls, and the thing is on him, its claws tearing at his thighs. His knife skids across the floor. Before he can reach for it a shadow fills the chamber.

The cave seems to spin as light radiates everywhere, finally coalescing into the torch held high by the second primitive who has just appeared in the chamber. The creature looks up. The second primitive raises a knife and with a cry drives it into the creature.

A deafening shriek as the thing sprawls backward. A moment and the primitive is upon it, driving the knife into it again and again as it tries to escape. With shocking strength and speed the creature throws the primitive to the cave floor.

Dazed, the primitive comes to his feet poised to attack, but the creature has vanished. He pauses, gasping for breath, and gazes down at his fallen companion. Blood soaks his garments, and his eyes are already clouded. He is dead. The primitive turns away, searching for his enemy. His eyes dart as he moves through the cave. In a nearby chamber he comes upon the fallen body of his enemy. Warily he approaches waving the torch at the creature's head. Slowly its eyes open. For a brief moment the gaze of the hunter and the hunted meet.

The primitive raises his knife to strike the final blow. Before his arm drops the creature swiftly attacks. In one motion the primitive drops the torch and with his other hand brings his knife forward, so that it slides through the creature's upper body. He withdraws it and stabs again, harder this time, while the creature writhes and the cavern resounds with its cries; he strikes it until it lies motionless upon the floor.

The primitive draws back, breathing hard, and leans upon his weapon. In front of him his prey lies dead.

Something black oozes from the creature's wounds. In the torchlight it seems to thicken and pool. As he stares at it, the primitive frowns.

There is a tiny fissure in the cavern floor. The black, oily substance moves toward it. Not naturally like water seeking its level, but like something alive. He watches, mesmerized, as the oil fills the crevice almost to overflowing, then disappears down the crack. It is several moments before he notices something else.

Across his chest are dark blots where the creature's blood has spattered him. The primitive's gaze is drawn to a single oily drop. He stares at it, brows furrowing. His expression changes, from annoyance to curiosity to horror. There are drops of black ooze everywhere upon him, crawling up his torso, along his arms, across the tops of his thighs, and over his chest. He grunts and begins brushing at them, but they will not move. He opens his mouth to scream but no sound comes out.

CHAPTER 1

BLACKWOOD, TEXAS
PRESENT DAY

Without warning a boy plunged through the roof of the cave.

"Stevie? Hey, Stevie—you okay?" a voice called from the opening above him. Three other boys stood there, peering nervously through the hole. For the last few days they'd been building a fort there, digging and hammering at the ground. Behind them, sun glared off the hard-baked earth. Miles to the east, the glittering contours of the Dallas skyline reared against the horizon. In the near-distance stretched a housing development, identical buildings scattered across a dun-colored landscape.

On the floor of the cave, Stevie lay winded. "I got—I got—I got the wind knocked out of me," he gasped at last.

Relieved laughter. Jason's face appeared alongside Jeremy's. "Looks like you were right, Stevie," he called down. "Looks like a cave or something."

Jeremy jostled the other boys, trying to get a better view. "What's down there, Stevie? Anything?"

Slowly Stevie got to his feet. He took a few unsteady steps. In the darkness something glistened, something round and smooth and roughly the size of a soccer ball. He picked it up and tilted it very carefully, so that the light struck it and it seemed to glow in his hands.

"Stevie?" Jeremy called again. "C'mon, what'd you find?"

"Human skull," breathed Stevie. "It's a human *skull!*"

Jason whooped. "Toss it up here, dude!"

Stevie shook his head. "No *way*, buttwipe. I found it. It's mine." He stood, looking around in amazement. "Holy cow. Anyways, there's bones all over the place down here."

He took a few steps back toward the pool of sunlight. He looked down, and saw that he was standing in some kind of oil slick. When he tried pulling his foot up, the ground sucked at the sole of his sneaker.

"Shit," he murmured, clutching the skull to him. "What the—"

And then he saw that the oil was everywhere, not just beneath his feet, but seeping up from cracks in the rock. And it was *moving*. Moving toward *him*. Black oil oozed up beneath his foot and wriggled down and into his sneaker. The skull fell from his hands and bounced across the stony floor as he tugged at his shorts and stared at the exposed skin of his leg.

Beneath the flesh something moved; a writhing thing as long as his finger. Only now there was more than one, there were dozens of them, all burrowing under his skin and moving upward. And there was something else, something just as frightening: where the black oil passed, his limbs were left feeling numb and frozen. Paralyzed.

"Stevie?" Jeremy stared down into the darkness. "Hey, Stevie?"

Stevie grunted but did not look up at him. Jeremy watched, unsure whether this was some kind of joke. "Stevie, you better not—"

"Stevie?" the other boys chimed in. "You okay?"

Stevie was definitely not okay. As they stared, Stevie's head fell backward so that he seemed to stare straight up at them, and in the glaring desert light they could see his eyes first filling with darkness and then turning completely, unnaturally black.

"Hey, man," whispered Jason. "Let's get outta here."

"Wait," said Jeremy. "We should help him—"

Jason and the other boy pulled him away. Jeremy went with them reluctantly, his footsteps echoing loudly against the dusty ground.

Sirens wailed counterpoint to the rush of wind over the plain. In the housing development doors slammed as people began to file onto their front steps a few at a time. At the end of one driveway, a spare figure in jeans and dark T-shirt hugged her arms as she scanned the horizon, then began to walk down the street out of the development.

The fire engines were already there. Two men in full rescue mode jumped from the hook-and-ladder vehicle, disengaged a ladder, and hurried toward the hole left by the boys. Several other men followed them as the captain pulled up in his car and hopped out, radio in hand.

"This is Captain Miles Cooles," he recited. "We've got a rescue situation in progress."

He stepped toward the hole. The three lead firemen had already slung the ladder down there, and one of them quickly stepped down it. His helmet gleamed in the sunlight, then winked from view as he reached the bottom and stepped away from the ladder.

"What you got down there, J.C.?" Cooles yelled after him. There was no response, and a moment later the second and third men followed the first into the darkness.

Outside, the sun beat mercilessly upon the growing circle of parents and children that had gathered. Captain Cooles stood silently, his weathered face taut with concern as he stared at the sinkhole. After a moment he sent two more men down.

Cooles glanced up sharply. A low ominous *whomp whomp* echoed through the torrid air, as a helicopter mysteriously materialized from the glowing sunset. Around him more and more people were slowly appearing, parents and children all staring at the western horizon. Faster than seemed possible the helicopter approached the huddled group, banked sharply, and then hovered above them. People clapped their palms over their ears and shaded their eyes as clouds of dust rose and the unmarked copter landed gently on the parched earth.

What the hell? thought Cooles. The helicopter's side door flew open, and five figures jumped out. Swathed in white Hazardous Materials suits, their faces hidden behind heavy masks, they carried a gleaming metal litter capped by a translucent plastic bubble, like an immense beetle carapace. They headed immediately for the hole. Cooles nodded and started after them, but before he had gone two paces another man debarked from the helicopter, a tall gaunt figure in white oxford-cloth shirt, his tie flapping in the propellers' backwash.

"Get those people back!" the man yelled, pointing to where the crowd was drifting curiously after the paramedics. A plastic tag round his neck identified him as DR.

BEN BRONSCHWEIG. "Get them out of here!"

Cooles nodded. He turned to the line of waiting firemen and shouted, "Move them all back! Now!" Then, hurrying to catch up with Bronschweig, he said, "I sent my men down after the boy. The report is that his eyes went black. That's the last I heard—"

Bronschweig ignored him and made a beeline for the sinkhole. Already the figures were clambering back up the ladder, bearing the limp body of the young boy on the bubble litter. At sight of this Bronschweig finally stopped, staring as the rescue crew bore it back toward the chopper. The crew followed, and as the gathered crowd watched in silence, the helicopter lifted back into the air, its blades sending billows of red dustlike smoke across the plain. A minute later and it was only a black smudge against the ruddy sky.

"Is that my boy?" a woman's voice asked from the back of the crowd. "Is that my boy?"

Bronschweig walked toward the development, Captain Cooles close behind. In the near distance a line of unmarked heavy vehicles barreled along the highway, turning into the access road leading to the little rows of identical houses. Unmarked cargo vans and squat trucks were driven by blank-faced men in dark uniforms. At the front of this threatening caravan were two huge white tanker trucks, devoid of any logo or advertising, gleaming ominously in the dying sun. Bronschweig stopped, arms crossed on his chest, and watched them with a tense expression.

"What about my men?" Captain Coole's loomed angrily at the doctor's side, his face red. "I sent five men down there—"

Bronschweig turned and walked away without a word.

Cooles waved furiously back at the sinkhole. "Goddamnit, did you hear what I said? I sent—"

Seeming not to hear him, Bronschweig walked toward the approaching trucks. A few of them had parked in a line in the cul-de-sac. Official-looking personnel were already pulling tents and tent poles, satellite dishes, banks of electric lights and monitoring equipment from them. The townspeople stared in bewilderment as the first of a myriad of refrigeration units were yanked from the backs of trucks and muscled toward the sinkhole. Drivers continued maneuvering the huge trucks, efficiently forming a barrier blocking the scene of action from the crowd's view.

Bronschweig disappeared into the melee. When he reached the tanker trucks he ducked between them and surreptitiously withdrew a cell phone. His face tight, he punched in a number, waited, and then spoke.

"Sir? The impossible scenario we hadn't planned for?" He listened for a moment, then replied tersely, "Well, we better come up with a plan."

CHAPTER 2

FEDERAL BUILDING
DALLAS, TEXAS

O ne week later, fifteen agents in dark windbreakers emblazoned with the letters FBI watched impassively as another helicopter hovered above them. They stood in seemingly random formation on a rooftop, their eyes

shielded by reflective sunglasses, faces uniformly expres-
sionless. At the sides of a half-dozen of them, leashed
Dobermans and German shepherds lolled exhausted,
tongues hanging out as they vainly sought relief from the
shimmering heat of midday. When the chopper touched
down, the dogs flattened their ears against their skulls, but
otherwise took no notice. A moment later the helicopter's
side door was flung open, and a single man emerged.
Hatchet-faced, his eyes narrowing as he took in the men
and women waiting on the roof, Special Agent-in-Charge
Darius Michaud paused, then walked authoritatively toward
them.

"We've evacuated the building and been through it bottom to top." One of the agents met him, cell phone in
hand, and motioned at the sweep of gray roof around them.
"No trace of an explosive device, or anything resembling
one."

Michaud looked at him, his mouth tight. "Have you
taken the dogs through?"

The agent nodded. "Yes, sir."

"Well, take them through again."

For an instant the agent stared at him, unable to hide
the weariness in his face. Then, "Yes, sir," he replied, and
turned back to his charges.

Behind him Michaud turned and scanned the horizon,
his hands linked behind his back. For a minute or two he
stood like this, registering the familiar silhouette of the
Dallas skyline, the flat silvery expanse of cloudless sky

beyond and the dull array of ladders and turbines and con-
crete atop the adjacent skyscraper.

Suddenly he stiffened. Shading his eyes with his
hand, he walked slowly to the edge of the roof, leaning
against the barrier there. He said nothing, but the line of
his mouth grew even tighter as he stared to where a solitary figure emerged from a door on the neighboring roof.
Even from this distance, he could see the resolve with
which the slender form moved beneath its FBI windbreaker, and the glint of sunlight on her shoulder-length
auburn hair. Michaud's hands clenched at the edge of the
wall.

On the other rooftop, Special Agent Dana Scully
winced as the door slammed shut behind her. Her finger
jabbed at her cell phone as she stepped carefully down the
stairs and onto the roof, looking around warily.

"Mulder?" she said urgently, the cell phone cool against
her cheek as she paused. "It's me."

Mulder's voice echoed tinnily in her ear. "Where are
you, Scully?"

"I'm on the roof."

"Did you find anything?"

She brushed a drop of sweat from her nose. "No. I
haven't."

"What's wrong, Scully?"

Scully drew herself up and shook her head impatiently,
as though Mulder stood in front of her and not somewhere
on the other end of a cell phone. "I've just climbed twelve

floors, I'm hot and thirsty and I'm wondering, to be honest, what I'm doing here."

"You're looking for a bomb," Mulder's unflappable voice replied.

Scully sighed. "I know that. But the threat was called in for the federal building across the street."

"I think they have that covered."

Scully grimaced even more impatiently. She took a deep breath and began, "Mulder, when a terrorist bomb threat is called in, the logical purpose of providing this information is to allow us to *find the bomb*. The rational object of terrorism is to provide terror. If you'd study the statistics, you'd find a model behavioral pattern in virtually every case where a threat has turned up an explosive device—"

She paused, and drew the cell phone closer, choosing her words as carefully as though she were explaining something to a rather slow, stolid child. "If we don't act in accordance with that data, Mulder—if you ignore it as we have done—the chances are great that if there actually *is* a bomb, we might not find it. Lives could be lost—"

She paused again for breath, and suddenly realized she'd been the only one talking for the last few minutes. Her voice rose slightly as she said, "Mulder . . . ?"

"What happened to playing a hunch?"

Scully almost jumped out of her skin: the voice came not from her cell phone but from two feet away. There, in the shadow of the AC unit, stood Fox Mulder. He raised an eyebrow almost imperceptibly as he cracked a sunflower seed between his teeth, tossing the spent husks to the ground as he clicked off his cell phone and stepped toward her.

"Jesus, Mulder!" Scully moaned, shaking her head.

"There's an element of surprise, Scully," said Mulder evenly. "Random acts of unpredictability."

He popped another sunflower seed into his mouth as he went on, "If we fail to anticipate the unforeseen or expect the unexpected in a universe of unforeseen possibilities, we find ourselves at the mercy of anyone or anything that cannot be programmed, categorized, or easily referenced. . . ."

As he spoke he walked toward the edge of the building. At the wall he leaned over, sailing his sunflower seeds off into the air and then dusting his hands off. For a moment he paused, staring thoughtfully, almost wistfully, into the nether distance, then turned to Scully and said, "What are we doing up here? It's hotter than hell."

And before Scully could make an exasperated reply he was off again, striding gracefully toward the stairs where Scully had emerged a few minutes before. She stood and watched him, then stuffed her cell phone into a pocket. Hiding a grin, she followed him, grabbing his arm and steering him up the steps.

"I know you're bored in this assignment," she said. Any faint vestige of humor leaked from her face. "But unconventional thinking is only going to get you into trouble now."

Mulder looked at her impassively. "How's that?"

"You've got to quit looking for what isn't there. They've closed the X-Files, Mulder. There's procedure to be followed here. *Protocol*," she added, giving the word a threatening emphasis.

Mulder nodded as though weighing her advice. Then, "What do you say we call in a bomb threat for Houston," he suggested, tilting his head to one side. "I think it's free beer night at the Astrodome."

Scully set her mouth and gave him a look, but it was no use. Sighing, she hurried past him up the stairs, took the last few steps until she stood at the top, and grabbed the doorknob. She twisted it, once, twice, futilely; and looked back at Mulder.

"Now what?" she demanded, her face grim.

Mulder's impish expression vanished. "It's locked?" he asked edgily.

Scully looked at him and wiggled the knob again. "So much for anticipating the unforeseen . . ."

She squinted up at the sun, then gazed at Mulder. Before she could say anything else, he lunged past her, yanking her hand from the knob. He turned it, and the door opened easily.

"Had you." Scully smirked, leaning against the wall.

Mulder shook his head. "No you didn't."

"Oh, yeah. Had you big time."

"No, you *didn't*—"

She slid past him into the stairwell, ignoring his protests as she headed for the freight elevator. She punched a button and waited for the welcoming *ping* as the doors opened.

"Sure did," she said smoothly, still grinning as Mulder shouldered into the elevator before her. "I saw your face, Mulder. There was a moment of panic."

Mulder stood with forced dignity as the elevator dropped. "Panic?" he said, and shook his head. "Have you ever seen me panic, Scully?"

The elevator drew to a halt. Refreshingly chill air pooled around them as the doors opened on to a busy lobby: suits with briefcases and sheaves of paper, delivery-men, uniformed couriers, and a bored-looking security guard.

"I just did," Scully said triumphantly as she sailed into the lobby. Before her a group of schoolchildren parted, heads turning excitedly at sight of her FBI jacket.

"When I panic, I make this face," said Mulder, staring at her completely deadpan.

Scully glanced at him. "Yeah, that's the face you made. You're buying."

Mulder followed her, heedless of the teacher now trying futilely to herd her charges into an adjoining elevator. "All right," he said reluctantly.

Scully stood with her arms crossed and stared pointedly at a door crowned by a sign that read SNACKS/BEVERAGES. Mulder dug in his pocket, fishing for change as he asked, "What'll it be? Coke, Pepsi? A saline IV?"

"Something sweet." She flashed a victory smile. Mulder

rolled his eyes and headed for the lounge. He walked slowly, sorting through a handful of change, as someone else elbowed by him on his way out of the room. A tall man in a blue vendor's uniform, hair close-cropped. His gaze passed briefly and casually over Mulder. Mulder glanced back, then hurried inside to catch the door before it closed.

Inside the windowless room he bypassed the ranks of snack and candy machines for a large, brightly lit monstrosity displaying soft drinks. He counted out the correct change and one by one plunked the coins through the slot, waiting for the reassuring *chunk* as each one hit bottom. Then he hit a button, leaned back on his heels, and—

Nothing.

"Oh, come *on*," groaned Mulder. He beat his fist against the front of the machine—still nothing—and finally rummaged through his pocket for more change. Slid it into the machine, stabbed the button—nothing.

"*Damn* it."

He stared at the cheerfully glowing display of cans, then pounded it with both fists; after a moment he gave one last jab at a button.

Nothing.

Swearing under his breath, Mulder stepped away from it, glared, then moved around to the back of the machine. There was perhaps a hand's-span of space between it and the wall. He crouched and peered there, frowning.

On the floor snaked a heavy black electrical cord. The plug lay a few inches from Mulder.

The machine wasn't plugged in.

He picked up the plug, stared at it with growing comprehension. Then, very quickly and very carefully he set it back onto the floor, and lightly stepped once more to the front of the machine he had just been pounding at. He opened the front panel and stared inside in horror. He grimaced at the memory of slamming his fist against the brightly lit surface, then turned and hurried to the door. He grabbed the knob, turned it—and met resistance.

"Shit," he murmured. He jiggled the knob, pulled on it, twisted it back and forth . . . but there was no longer a shred of doubt in his mind. He was locked in.

Frantically, he pulled out his cell phone and punched in a number, pressed the phone tight against his ear as he stared at the soda machine. A moment later Scully's voice filtered through the receiver.

"Scully."

Mulder took a deep breath. "Scully, I found the bomb."

Outside the vending room, Scully paced the lobby and rolled her eyes. "Where are you, Mulder?"

"I'm in the vending room."

She nodded to herself, glanced down a short corridor, and headed down it. When she heard faint pounding she turned and found herself facing a door.

SNACKS/REFRESHMENTS

"Is that you pounding?" she questioned, and tentatively turned the knob.

On the other side, Mulder cupped the phone against his

chin and pounded even harder. "Scully, get someone to open this door."

Scully shook her head. "Nice try, Mulder."

Mulder twisted away from the door and started pulling at the front of the soda machine. "Scully, listen to me." A desperate edge crept into his voice as the hinged front of the machine swung open. "It's in the Coke machine. You've got about fourteen minutes to get this building evacuated."

Scully shook her head. She tried the door again—still locked. Losing patience, she said, "C'mon. Open the door."

Her response met with even more hard pounding. For the first time, Scully felt a spark of fear. "Mulder?" she breathed into the cell phone. "Tell me this is a joke."

Mulder's voice echoed in her ear. "Thirteen fifty-nine, thirteen fifty-eight, thirteen fifty-seven . . ." As he intoned, Scully bent to examine the keyhole beneath the door's metal knob.

It had been soldered over. She pressed her thumb against it, felt the faintest warmth and pressure—recent work.

". . . thirteen fifty-six . . . Do you see a pattern emerging here, Scully?"

"Hang on," said Scully. "I'm gonna get you out of there."

Inside the vending room, Mulder's phone went dead. He snapped it closed and shoved it back into his pocket, then squatted in front of the soda machine. Inside was a battery of circuit boards and snaking wires, digital readouts and row after row of clear plastic canisters filled with fluid hooked up to what had to be bricks of plastique. In the middle of all this a blinking LED display registered the countdown. Mulder stared at it, fighting dread, and thought, *It's gonna take an expert a lot longer than thirteen minutes to figure out where to even start on this. . . .*

In the building lobby, Scully strode up to the security desk, barking orders as she swept her arm out to indicate the oblivious crowd of office workers.

"I need this building evacuated and cleared out in ten minutes!" She stabbed at the air in front of the security chief and yelled, "I need you to get on the phone and tell the fire department to block off the city center in a one mile radius around the building."

The security chief gaped. "In *ten minutes?*"

"DON'T THINK!" shouted Scully. "JUST PICK UP THE PHONE AND MAKE IT HAPPEN!"

But people in the lobby were already running out and she was gone before he could protest or command an expla-nation, already dialing another number on her phone.

"This is Special Agent Dana Scully. I need to speak to S.A.C. Michaud. He's got the wrong building—"

She stopped beside the front revolving doors and stared out to where anonymous vans and cars were suddenly screeching up to the curb. Agents in FBI windbreakers ran from the unmarked vehicles, Darius Michaud among them.

"Where is it?" he demanded as he rushed into the lobby to meet Scully. Around them workers streamed out of the building, their voices high-pitched with anxiety. The school-teacher shouted as she hurried her class past, the children crying out excitedly when the saw the mob of FBI agents. Scully paused and stared out the huge glass wall, to where fire engines roared up alongside the unmarked vans, followed by a phalanx of city buses. Everything suddenly had the feel of a situation that was verging out of control.

She caught herself before she could give in to that desperate line of thought and turned to face Michaud. "Mulder found it in a vending machine. He's locked in with it."

Michaud looked over his shoulder and yelled at an agent directing people through the doors. "Get Kesey with the torch! It's in the vending room."

He looked back at Scully. "Take me there," he commanded.

"This way—"

The windowless room felt like a cell to Mulder, as he crouched in front of the soda machine and stared glassy-eyed at the array of explosives there, the shifting pattern of red numerals on the LED display.

7:00

He wiped a bead of sweat from his chin, hurriedly punched at his cell phone as it began to chime. He jumped, then switched the phone on with relief.

"Scully? You know that face I was making—I'm making it now."

"Mulder." Scully's voice was muffled by a keening sound in the hallway. "Move away from the door. We're coming through it."

He backed away, even as the brilliant blue-white flame of a gas plasma torch began to roughly trace the outline of the metal door. Gray smoke sifted inside as the stench of scorched metal filled the room. The hinges glowed, then turned black. The torch finished its circuit of the doorway, so that a somewhat smaller rectangle momentarily appeared within it. Mulder heard a series of thumps and a faint voice yelling "Go!" Then, with a muted crash, the door fell inward and crashed to the floor.

"Mulder . . ." Scully began, but was silenced as Michaud shoved past her, handing off the plasma torch to another agent and grabbing a hefty tool kit. She followed him inside, along with three other agents—bomb techs. They headed for where Mulder stood gazing at the soda machine's digital readout.

4:07

Mulder shook his head. "Tell me that's just soda pop in those canisters."

Michaud gingerly set the tool kit on the floor and

stooped in front of the machine. "No. It's what it looks like. A big I.E.D.—ten gallons of astrolite."

He pursed his lips, studying the bomb, and without looking up, commanded, "Okay. Get everybody out of here and clear the building."

Mulder frowned. "Somebody's got to stay here with you."

"I gave you an order," Michaud snapped, still not looking up. "Now get the hell out of here and evacuate the area."

Scully sidled up behind him. "Can you defuse it?"

"I think so." Michaud snapped the tool kit open and withdrew a pair of wire clippers. The other agents nodded at each other and quickly left the room.

Michaud pushed up the sleeves of his windbreaker and flexed the wire clippers. Mulder watched him dubiously.

"You've got about four minutes to find out if you're wrong."

Without warning Michaud turned on him. "Did you hear what I said?" His voice shook slightly, and there was a febrile intensity to his gaze.

"Let's go, Mulder," Scully murmured. "Come on."

She started out the door. Mulder remained for a moment longer, staring at Michaud.

But the other man's attention was focused solely on the bomb. Seconds passed, until finally Mulder turned and followed Scully into the corridor. In the room behind him Michaud set the wire clippers carefully on his knee but did nothing else; only crouched staring at the bomb. Just staring.

Outside, the last of the building's occupants had been evacuated. The horde of schoolchildren raced up the steps of one of the city buses, while other buses pulled away from the curb in clouds of exhaust. People ran pell-mell across the plaza, headed for the relative safety of the far side of the street, where police barricades had been hastily erected, and where uniformed men frantically directed the last stragglers to flee.

"Go, *now!*" bullhorns howled, and their echo rang out above the cries and shouting of the panicking mob.

The plaza in front of the building was all but empty now. As the last buses roared off, the fire engines did the same, and the police cars, until only a single police car and one anonymous sedan remained, engines running, at curbside. The revolving doors *whooshed* as Scully and Mulder raced out, heading across the plaza to the waiting cars. Abruptly Mulder slowed, then stopped. He shaded his eyes and stared back at the building.

"What are you doing?" Scully had gone on ahead, but suddenly noticed his hesitation. "Mulder?"

A solitary figure in FBI windbreaker burst from the revolving door: the last man out.

"All clear!" he shouted, his footsteps echoing as he ran toward the idling cop car. Mulder ignored him and remained staring as though entranced by the building.

"Something's wrong. . . ."

Scully hurried to his side. *"Mulder?"*

The cop car zoomed away. In the sole remaining vehicle, an FBI agent gazed in disbelief at Mulder, then yelled, "What's he doing?!"

"Something's not right," Mulder said, as though to himself. Scully shook her head and grabbed his arm.

"Mulder! Get in the car!" In the waiting vehicle the agent motioned at them furiously. "There's no time, Mulder!"

She pulled him after her, heading for the car. Mulder twisted to stare over his shoulder.

"Michaud . . ." he said.

In the vending room, Michaud had replaced the wire clippers and shut his tool chest. Now he was sitting on it, his eyes fixed on the LED display.

:30

He watched as the seconds disappeared, yet still did nothing. Finally he let his head drop forward against his chest, not so much in despair as resignation, a devoted Bureau man to the last.

Outside the sun beat heedlessly upon the nearly empty plaza.

"Mulder!" Scully shouted, and at last he relented, hurrying alongside her to the car.

"For chrissakes, get in," urged the agent standing in the open door of the driver's side. "It's going to go at any second—"

Mulder slid into the backseat, Scully into the front, and the car peeled off. They turned to gaze out the rear window, watching as the building receded—ten yards, twenty, not quickly enough.

And suddenly it exploded, the entire edifice consumed by a immense ball of flame that ripped up from the bottom floor, expanding until it seemed to devour everything in sight. Smoke surged outward along with buckling steel girders and rippling waves of broken glass, and the air thundered deafeningly. Scully cried out but her voice was swallowed by that terrible roar, her arm bashed against the car door as the bomb's impact traveled through the air and sent the car caroming across the plaza, slamming against the back of a car parked on the street. It lifted up in the back and then slammed back down; all around them other cars did the same. There was a sharp *crack*, and the rear window collapsed into granular particles of safety glass, showering the two of them.

"You okay?" bellowed the agent from the front seat.

"I-I think so," Scully gasped.

Outside shards of glass were everywhere. The air seethed with blackened debris, ash and metal and burning plastic. As Mulder and Scully watched, horrified, the entire side of the building emerged from the smoke, so that they

31

could see inside to where flames raced along abandoned corridors and through the ravaged remains of cubicles and offices. From ground floor to rooftop fires raged, and in the distance the first sirens began to wail.

In the backseat Mulder shook his head, dispersing glittering bits of safety glass. Slowly he leaned out the broken side window to open the door. He got out while Scully exited the front, the two of them shaken and breathless as they looked up at the burning building, broken glass, and fluttering bits of flaming paper cascading everywhere.

"Next time, *you're* buying," he said darkly.

CHAPTER 3

FBI HEADQUARTERS
J. EDGAR HOOVER BUILDING
WASHINGTON, D.C.
ONE DAY LATER

T he sign on the door read OFFICE OF PROFESSIONAL REVIEW. Inside Scully shifted nervously in her chair, far too conscious that the one beside her was empty, and tried to focus on what was being said.

"In light of Waco, and Ruby Ridge . . ."

Scully bit her lip. This review was important, far too important for Mulder to be late; but Scully herself had barely made it here on time, exhausted as she was by the night-owl from Dallas back to D.C. In front of her, six assistant directors were arranged at a long table, shuffling papers and clearing their throats self-importantly. At the center of the conference table Assistant Director Jana Cassidy was declaiming, with the air of someone who held the fate of the world in her strong, impeccably manicured hands.

". . . for the catastrophic destruction of public property and the loss of life due to terrorist activities . . ."

Next to Cassidy, Assistant Director Walter Skinner cast Scully a level look, letting his gaze linger for just a moment upon Mulder's conspicuously empty chair. Over the years Skinner had spent a lot of time in this room. Scully and Mulder reported directly to him, and had since they'd been working together. When he could get away with it, he'd acted as something of a champion for Mulder and Scully. That would be difficult this morning, though, with Mulder absent. Scully crossed and uncrossed her legs, and tried not to glance over her shoulder again at the door.

"Many details are still unclear," said Cassidy. Her cool blue eyes regarded Scully from above a sheaf of papers as she went on pointedly. "Some agents' reports have not been filed, or have come in sketchy, without a satisfactory accounting of the events that led to the destruction in Dallas. But we're under some pressure to give an accurate picture of what happened to the Attorney General, so she can issue a public statement."

And then Scully heard what she'd been waiting for: the muted creak of the door finally opening and a familiar foot-step. She turned to see Mulder, his freshly pressed suit jacket doing a poor job of hiding the fact that he wore the same shirt he'd had on yesterday, his face creased with the slightly chagrined expression of a man who knows he's late for his own funeral. Scully didn't dare smile, but she felt her heart lift as Mulder pulled out the chair beside her. He said noth-ing, acknowledging her with a glance before turning his attention to Cassidy. The keen-eyed lawyer turned and glared sternly at the two of them, and continued before Mulder could sit.

"We know now that five people died in the explosion. Special Agent-in-Charge Darius Michaud, who was trying to defuse the bomb that had been hidden inside a vending machine. Three firemen from Dallas, and a young boy."

Mulder's hand froze on the chair in front of him. He looked quickly at Scully, who's raised eyebrow confirmed that this was news to her, too.

"Excuse me—" Mulder shook his head, trying to keep his voice even as he questioned Cassidy. "The firemen and the boy—they were in the building?"

Cassidy's cool gaze grew icy. "Agent Mulder, since you weren't able to be on time for this meeting, I'm going to ask you to step back outside, so that we can get Agent Scully's version of the facts. So that she won't have to be paid the same disrespect that you're showing the rest of us."

Mulder stared her down unflinchingly. "We were told the building was clear."

"You'll get your turn, Agent Mulder." Cassidy's frigid tone held a warning as she gestured at the door. "Please step out."

Mulder swallowed, and for first time looked over at the other ADs at the table. The only sympathetic face he found was Skinner's, but Skinner's sympathy was tempered with a warning. The assistant director had been here with Mulder on many occasions, and watched as the younger man inevitably ran up against the Bureau and its stiff conventions. There wasn't much that Skinner could do for Mulder, stuck as he was in the middle of it all; and right now it seemed unlikely that he'd be able to do anything at all.

But it was always worth a try. Mulder fought to keep his voice even, and motioned at the binder in front of Jana Cassidy.

"It does say there in your paperwork that Agent Scully and I were the ones who found the bomb. . . ."

Cassidy sternly waved him off. "Thank you, Agent Mulder. We'll call you back in shortly."

Defeated, Mulder slid his chair back and left the room. Scully watched him go. A moment later, Walter Skinner quietly excused himself and followed Mulder into the hallway.

He found the younger agent standing in front of a display case, staring broodingly at the marksmanship trophies inside.

"Sit down," said Skinner, indicating a beige couch beside the case. "It'll be a few minutes. They're still talking to Agent Scully."

Mulder plopped onto the couch, and Skinner joined him. "About what?"

"They're asking her for a narrative. They want to know why she was in the wrong building."

"She was with me."

Skinner studied Mulder, shaking his head. "You don't see what's going on, do you?" he said softly. "There's forty million dollars in damage to the city of Dallas. Lives have been lost. No suspects have been named. So the story being shaped is that *this could have been prevented*. That the FBI didn't do its job."

Mulder's eyes narrowed. "And they want to blame us?"

"Agent Mulder, we both know that if you and Agent Scully hadn't taken the initiative to search the adjacent building, we could have multiplied those fatalities by a hundred—"

"But it's not the lives we saved." Mulder paused, savoring the irony. "It's the lives we didn't."

Skinner shot him a mirthless smile, and recited the dictum, "If it looks bad, it's bad for the FBI."

Mulder's hand clenched. "If they want someone to blame, they can blame me. Agent Scully doesn't deserve this."

"She's in there right now saying the same thing about you."

Mulder shook his head. "I breached protocol. I broke contact with the SAC. . . ."

He paused, remembering Michaud's drawn face as he stared at the explosive-rigged vending machine, and blinked painfully at the image. "I—I ignored a primary tactical rule and left him alone with the device. . . ."

"Agent Scully says it was she who ordered you out of the building. That you wanted to go back—"

"Look, she was—"

Before he could on, the door opened. The two men looked up to see Scully exiting. The look she gave Mulder told him that, whatever had happened inside the Professional Review Office, it hadn't gone well. She took a deep breath, then stepped briskly to where the men sat.

"They've asked for you, sir," she said, indicating Skinner.

Skinner gave one last look at Mulder. Then he stood and, thanking Scully, returned to the review. Scully watched the door close behind him, her expression pained. Mulder stared at her and after a moment said, "Whatever you told them in there, you don't have to protect me."

Scully shook her head. "All I told them was the truth." Her deep blue eyes looked wounded, but she avoided his gaze.

"They're trying to divide us on this, Scully." Mulder's voice rose defensively. "We can't let them."

For the first time Scully gazed directly at her partner.

"They *have* divided us, Mulder. They're splitting us up."

On the couch Mulder stared back at her, uncomprehendingly. Finally he said, "What? What are you talking about?"

"I meet with OPR day after tomorrow for remediation and reassignment."

Mulder looked stricken. "Why?"

Sighing, Scully sank onto the couch. "I think you must have an idea. They cited a history of problems relating back to 1993."

"But they were the ones who put us together—" Mulder protested heatedly.

"Because they wanted me to invalidate your work," Scully interrupted, "your investigations into the paranormal. But I think this goes deeper than that. . . ."

"This isn't about you, Scully." Mulder stared at her intensely, almost pleadingly. "They're doing this to *me.*"

"*They're* not doing this, Mulder." Scully looked away, avoiding his gaze. "I left behind a career in medicine because I thought I might make a difference at the FBI. When they recruited me, they told me that women made up nine percent of the Bureau. I felt that was not an impediment, but an opportunity to distinguish myself.

"But it hasn't turned out that way. And now, even if I were to be transferred to Omaha, or Wichita, or some other field office where I'm sure I could rise—it just doesn't hold the interest for me it once did. Not after what I've seen and done."

She fell silent, and stared at her hands. Beside her Mulder sat in disbelief.

"You're . . . quitting?"

For a moment Scully said nothing. Finally she shrugged. "There's really no reason left for me to stay anymore. . . ."

She turned then, gazing at Mulder with frank blue eyes. "Maybe you should ask yourself if your heart's still in it, too."

Behind them the door to the hearing room creaked open. Mulder looked up, his expression still stunned as he saw Walter Skinner standing in the corridor, gesturing to him.

"Agent Mulder. You're up."

Scully looked at him sadly. "I'm sorry," she said softly. "Good luck."

He turned to her, waiting to see if there would be more, giving her the chance to change her mind, to offer a better explanation, anything. But Scully said nothing else. At last Mulder stood, his stunned expression giving way to something like despair, and followed Skinner into the office. Scully watched him go. Before he reached the door, she called his name. When Mulder turned, she picked up the jacket he'd forgotten on the chair. He walked over, and she handed it to him.

Only after the door shut behind him did she let her resolve fade, and gave voice to a sigh that was almost like a sob.

CHAPTER

4

CASEY'S BAR
SOUTHEAST WASHINGTON, D.C.

C asey's never got much of a crowd on a weeknight. A few regulars, government employees who wandered over from the Mall to knock back a few before catching the last Metro back to Falls Church or Silver

Spring or Bethesda. Mulder had been here since late after-noon, and the bartender was wondering if he was ever going to leave.

"I'd say this just about exceeds your minimum daily requirement," she said, pouring a jolt of tequila into a shot glass in front of him. She smiled, brushing back a strand of faded blond hair, and replaced the bottle.

In front of her, Fox Mulder sat by himself on a stool. He stared at the sticky rings on the bar's dark wood surface, the dull light gilding the edges of four empty shot glasses. When the bartender placed the full glass in front of him he spun it thoughtfully, licking his finger where a drop of tequila had spilled, before tossing back the shot. When he put it back down, he drunkenly knocked over the other glasses.

"Gotta train for this kind of heavy lifting," she went on, eyeing him with some concern—this guy definitely did not seem like he'd been practicing much before tonight.

Mulder tilted his head as though considering her advice, then motioned for another shot. She retrieved the empty glasses, intrigued by his brooding silence.

"Poopy day?" she ventured.

"Yup." Mulder's voice sounded thick and out of prac-tice.

"A woman?" He shook his head. "Work?"

Mulder nodded and the barmaid looked sympathetic, but that changed when he pointed to the tequila bottle again.

"You sure?" she asked. He stared fixedly at the bottle, and she reluctantly poured another shot. Mulder drank it, shuddering a little as the liquor scored his throat. Then he banged the glass on the bar, half-turned on his stool, and closed his eyes as a wave of dizziness swept over him. When he opened them an instant later he saw another man staring at him from the end of the bar. An older man, early sixties perhaps, with a broad, weathered face and wearing an old Brooks Brothers summer suit, crumpled linen and the same color as the few gray hairs at the man's temples. Mulder stared at him blearily and incuriously, then turned back to the bar.

"Another."

She poured it, then began gathering the empty shots and placing them in a plastic basin. "What do you do?"

"What do I do?" Mulder looked up at her and nodded. "I'm a key figure in an ongoing government charade. An annoyance to my superiors. A joke among my peers. They call me 'Spooky.' Spooky Mulder . . ."

Whose sister was abducted by aliens when he was a kid. Who now chases little green men with a badge and a gun, shouting to the heavens and anyone else who'll listen that the fix is in. . . .

The bartender's sympathetic expression was fading. What a freak, her restrained silence implied.

"That our government's hip to the truth and a part of the conspiracy. That the sky is falling, and when it hits it's gonna be the shit storm of all time."

He finished and flashed her a bitter smile. She stared back at him, then quickly pulled back the shot she'd just poured.

"I think that just about does it, Spooky." She dumped the tequila in the sink and began writing up a check.

"Does what?"

"Looks like eighty-six is your lucky number."

Mulder looked at her sadly. Nobody believed him. "One is the loneliest number."

She shook her head and decisively placed the check in front of him. "Too bad. Closing time for you."

Mulder shrugged impassively and slid off the stool. He tottered a little, and instinctively glanced around to see if anyone had noticed. But the bartender had already turned away, and the older man at the other end of the rail was gone. Mulder took a step toward the front door, remembered the check, and turned. He dropped a small wad of bills on the bar counter and walked unsteadily toward the back of the room, where a dim, narrow hallway led to the bathrooms. A piece of paper was thumbtacked to the men's room door.

OUT OF ORDER.

"Shit," muttered Mulder.

He rattled the door to the adjoining women's room—an irritated voice responded.

"Sorry," Mulder said hastily. Gathering what was left of his wits, he turned and stumbled back down the corridor, to where a fire door opened out onto the alley, and went outside.

A row of Dumpsters reared up against a crumbling brick wall. Mulder found a space between two of them and unzipped his fly. Moments later he started as a voice came from behind him.

"That official FBI business?"

"*What?*"

"Bet the Bureau's accusing you of doing the same thing in Dallas."

Mulder stiffened drunkenly as a figure emerged from the shadows: the same older man in the rumpled linen suit who'd been observing him inside the bar. The stranger gave him a crooked smile and eased himself unthreateningly into a space a few yards from where Mulder stood.

"How's that?" asked Mulder cautiously.

"Standing around holding your yank while bombs are exploding."

The stranger laughed as Mulder turned and eyed him. "Do I know you?"

"No. But I've been watching your career for a good while. Back when you were just a promising young agent. Before that . . ."

"You follow me out here for a reason?"

"Yeah. I did." The man turned so that his back was to Mulder and unzipped his own pants. "My name's Kurtzweil. Dr. Alvin Kurtzweil."

Mulder frowned, trying to ignore the intrusion. He zipped himself up and turned around, ready to leave.

"Old friend of your father's." Kurtzweil looked over his

shoulder and smiled at Mulder's bewildered expression. "Back at the Department of State. We were what you might call fellow travelers, but his disenchantment outlasted mine." Kurtzweil waited, as though giving Mulder the chance to let this all sink in.

Mulder's expression grew stony. Quickly he took the last few steps to the door and jerked it open.

Kurtzweil finished heeding nature's call, zipped up, and followed Mulder inside. He caught up with him at the coat rack by the door, where the younger man was fumbling with his jacket.

"How'd you find me?" Mulder asked. He sounded more weary than angry.

Kurtzweil shrugged. "Heard you come here now and again. Figured you'd be needing a little drinky tonight . . ."

"You a reporter?"

Kurtzweil shook his head and took his own raincoat from the rack. "I'm a doctor, but I think I mentioned that. OB-GYN."

"Who sent you?"

"I came on my own. After reading about the bombing in Dallas."

Mulder stared at him measuringly, taking in Kurtzweil's rheumy, intelligent eyes and wry mouth. "Well, if you've got something to tell me, you've got as long as it takes for me to hail a cab," he said, and started out the door.

Before he could hit the sidewalk, Kurtzweil grabbed his arm. "They're going to pin Dallas on you, Agent

46

Mulder." His tone was not accusatory. If anything, he sounded apologetic, even sorrowful—the trusted family retainer bringing news of a death. "But there was nothing you could've done. Nothing *anyone* could've done to prevent that bomb from going off—

"Because the truth is something you'd never have guessed. Never even have predicted."

Mulder stared at him, his face twisting into rage. He pulled away and stormed down the sidewalk as Kurtzweil followed him doggedly. "And what's that?" Mulder snapped.

Kurtzweil hurried until he was alongside him. "S.A.C. Darius Michaud never tried or intended to defuse the bomb."

Mulder paused, teetering on the edge of the curb. Around them L'Enfant Plaza was a wasteland of rain-slicked streets and empty newspaper machines. In the near-distance ugly government buildings loomed, and a few Yellow Cabs hopefully trolled Constitution Avenue for customers. Mulder looked around in disgust, turned to Kurtzweil, and said in rhetorical disbelief, "He just let it explode."

Kurtzweil tugged at the collar of his raincoat. "What's the question nobody's asking? Why *that* building? Why not the federal building?"

Mulder looked pained. "The federal building was too well guarded—"

"*No.*" Kurtzweil's voice grew agitated as Mulder stepped

into the street, raising his hand to hail a cab. "They put the bomb in the building across the street because it *did* have federal offices. The Federal Emergency Management Agency had a provisional medical quarantine office there. Which is where the bodies were found. But *that's* the thing—"

The taxi pulled over. Kurtzweil sidestepped a puddle as he followed Mulder to its side. "—the thing you didn't know. That you'd never think to check."

Mulder was already pulling the door open, lowering himself to slide inside. Kurtzweil gazed at him, his eyes no longer sad but fierce, almost challenging. "Those people were already dead."

Mulder blinked. "Before the bomb went off?"

"That's what I'm saying."

Mulder stared at him for a moment. He shook his head. "Michaud was a twenty-two-year veteran of the Bureau—"

"Michaud was a patriot. The men he's loyal to know their way around Dallas. They blew away that building to hide something. Maybe something even they couldn't pre-dict."

Kurtzweil leaned against the cab and looked at Mulder, waiting. The younger man shook his head, no longer quite disbelieving but as though slowly teasing out the answer to a puzzle. "You're saying they destroyed an entire building to hide the bodies of three firemen?"

Kurtzweil banged the top of the cab triumphantly—the right answer at last! "*And* one little boy."

Without a word, Mulder got into the cab and slammed the door. He looked at the driver. "Take me to Arlington." He rolled down the window and stared up at Kurtzweil.

"I think you're full of shit," he said.

"Do you?" Kurtzweil asked evenly. He rapped the taxi's roof and stepped away, watching as it sped away. "Do you really, Agent Mulder?" he repeated to himself thoughtfully.

Inside the cab, Mulder leaned forward, frowning. "I changed my mind," he said to the driver. "I want to go to Georgetown."

Dana Scully lay in bed, staring at the ceiling. Despite her exhaustion, she hadn't been able to sleep; hadn't been able to do anything, really, but lie there and endlessly replay the events of the last two days: the explosion in Dallas and its aftermath, the interminable meeting that had led to the termination of her career with the Federal Bureau of Investigation. Outside the rain beat at the windows, a noise that she normally found reassuring, but which tonight sounded only like another reprimand, another reminder that somehow she had come up short, in the Bureau's estimation and—what was even worse—her own.

And Mulder's. At the thought of her partner, Scully sighed and closed her eyes, fighting back a despair that went even deeper than tears. It didn't even bear thinking about, that this was the end of it—

Don't go there, a voice echoed inside her skull, trying to put a wry spin on it. But Scully only bit her lip.

I'm there, she thought.

The rain battered the walls of her apartment, the wind sent branches rattling against the roof; and then she heard something else. She sat up bolt upright, cocking her head.

Someone was pounding at the door. Scully glanced at her bedside clock. 3:17. She grabbed her bathrobe and hurried into the living room. At the door she hesitated, listening to whoever was on the other side pause, then begin to bang even harder. She peeked through the peephole, stepped back, and sighed, her relief tinged with annoyance. Then she removed the safety chain, unlocked the door, and pulled it open.

Mulder stood there, his clothes wet and hair disheveled. Despite his disarray, and the hour, he looked strangely, even disturbingly, alert.

"I wake you?"

Scully shook her head. "No."

"Why not?" Mulder breezed past her into the apartment. As he did she caught the sweet-sour reek of tequila and the fainter, stale smoky scent that all bars have at closing time. "It's three A.M.—"

She closed the door and stared at him in disbelief. "Are you *drunk*, Mulder?"

"I was until about twenty minutes ago."

Scully crossed her arms against her chest and stared at

him coolly. "Is that before or after you got the idea to come here?"

Mulder looked puzzled. "What are you implying, Scully?"

"I thought you may have gotten drunk and decided to come here to talk me out of quitting."

"Is that what you'd like me to do?"

Scully shut her eyes and leaned against the wall. Recalling how fifteen minutes ago, an hour ago, she had been thinking exactly that. After a moment she opened her eyes and sighed. "Go home, Mulder. It's late."

He shook his head, with a resolute, slightly manic gleam in his eyes. A look Scully knew all too well and usually to her peril. He reached down to pick up her windbreaker, still lying on the couch where she'd dropped it last night, and held it out to her. "Get dressed, Scully."

"Mulder, what are you *doing*?"

"Just get dressed," he said. The manic gleam grew even more intense, but it couldn't hide the beginning of a grin, the slightest hint that something big was afoot. "I'll explain on the way."

CHAPTER 5

BLACKWOOD, TEXAS

The night breeze swept across the prairie relentlessly. After a while the wind seemed to rise, as though heavy weather was moving in.

Above the desolation of sage and dust, two black, unmarked helicopters appeared, swooping perilously close to the ground.

They buzzed past, flying at dangerously low altitude toward their destination: several large, ominously glowing domes, duplicates of the moon's own reflection upon the prairie. Only a few hundred yards away, the commonplace lights of the housing development sparked the night, white and yellow and ice-blue where a television was on. But there was nothing commonplace about the work site that had sprung up where, only days before, four young boys had knelt digging in the brick-colored earth.

Now, the white hoods of several geodesic dome tents stretched over nearly the entire patch of ground. They were surrounded by long white cargo trucks, their tanks devoid of any markings, and a number of anonymous support vehicles: cars, vans, pickup trucks. Between these, figures in black fatigues moved purposefully, their somber uniforms in stark contrast to the white Hazardous Materials suits worn by their counterparts who stepped in and out of the central dome and support tents.

Overhead the hum of the choppers became a drone, as the two aircraft banked and then slowly settled upon the ground. Dust devils spun up around them; tents billowed and tugged at their struts. The eerie daylight glow of the main dome washed over one of the helicopters, as several men in fatigues gestured at the pilot. An instant later and the chopper's door swung open. A man stepped down, moving with studied, almost casual ease as he shielded his eyes from the dust and blinding light. He lowered his head instinctively as he walked beneath the whirring propellers, heading to where a line of trucks provided a makeshift windbreak from the helicopter's prop wash. Once there, he stood with his back to it all—choppers, drones, the huge and weirdly glowing tent—and lit a cigarette.

"Sir?"

The Cigarette-Smoking Man replaced his light and inhaled, then turned to look at the uniformed man addressing him. "Dr. Bronschweig is waiting for you in the main staging area."

The Cigarette-Smoking Man regarded him through slit eyes, his weathered face dull gray in the dome's glare. His expression was cool, almost disinterested, but after a moment he nodded and without a word followed the other man across the field. At the entrance to the central dome, the uniformed man nodded curtly, indicating the bulky white form of someone in a Haz-Mat suit. "Dr. Smith will escort you inside," he said, and left.

"This way, sir." From behind his mask the man's voice sounded hollow and thin. He held open a vinyl flap, and the Cigarette-Smoking Man ducked beneath.

Inside, the dome was a maze of clear plastic tubing, translucent vinyl walls, and opaque barriers separating one work area from another. In between, in makeshift cubicles and plastic-sided alleys, men and women stood or sat before stainless steel tables. Some wore Haz-Mat suits or surgical masks; all had the intense, almost dreamy expressions of people engaged in work they had spent a lifetime preparing for. The tables were covered with vials and alembics and crucibles of glass, but also with homelier instruments: hammers, chisels, sifters, and strainers, all the accoutrements of the archaeologist's art. The entire place resembled a cross between a high-tech dig and a surgical operating theater.

Or a modern abattoir. There were refrigeration units everywhere, huge and linked by sheaves of electrical cords. The dome resonated with their humming, and the faint sweetish smell they exuded. The Cigarette-Smoking Man passed them quickly and in silence, barely taking note of the hive of activity around him, until finally he came to the entrance to the very center of the dome. Here he took the bulky white suit and mask that an underling handed him, donning it quickly before drawing aside the last vinyl flap and entering.

Inside was a small, partitionless area, banked round-about with refrigeration units. It was cold, cold enough that the Cigarette-Smoking Man's breath clouded even inside his mask. Several metal gurneys were tucked beneath halogen lights and shrouds of plastic sheathing. In the middle of it all, a small mound of bare earth had been covered by a clear plastic cover, like a manhole cover: twelve inches thick, its transparent surface crisscrossed by heavy stainless steel bars. The walls of the earthen hole had been shored up by inserting a sort of metal tube into the ground, like a culvert, big enough for a man to pass through. It was this that the sturdy cover fit over, like a trapdoor. And it was from this entrance into the underworld that Dr. Bronschweig appeared, suited up, his head obscured by the cumbersome mask. He pushed aside the clear plastic hatch and stepped out as the Cigarette-Smoking Man approached him.

"You've got something to show me."

Dr. Bronschweig nodded. Not even his mask could hide his excited expression, or the nervous tone edging his voice. "Yes."

He pointed to the hatch, the ladder that could be glimpsed now leading into the earth. The Cigarette-Smoking Man slung himself down the hole, moving awkwardly in his suit as he went down the ladder. A moment later Dr. Bronschweig followed.

They were inside the cave, a frigid chamber lit by an array of halogen and fluorescent lights. "We brought the atmosphere here back down to freezing in order to control the development," he explained. "And that development is like nothing we've ever seen. . . ."

The Cigarette-Smoking Man stood beside him, catching his breath. "Brought on by what?"

"Heat, I think. The coincident invasion of a host—the fireman—and an environment that raised his body temperature above 98.6."

He motioned the other man to follow him to one end of the cavern. Two portable drilling rigs had been set up on the floor, their pistons moving silently up and down, like macabre rocking horses. Behind them, more plastic sheets hung from the ceiling, to form an eerily glowing drapery of cool blue lit from within. Dr. Bronschweig hesitated, then pushed away the plastic.

"Here—"

The flickering blue light revealed a gurney, draped with the ubiquitous plastic but differing from the others the Cigarette-Smoking Man had seen in one regard:

There was a body on it. A man, unclothed, his body covered with a filigree of tubes and cords and wires that led to a battery of monitors lined up against the cavern wall. There was a muted drone as the equipment registered his vital signs, the rhythmic pulse and sigh of respirators and the metronomic beat of a cardiac ventilator monitoring his heartbeat. The Cigarette-Smoking Man quietly stared down at its occupant.

"This man's still alive," he said. He stared at the body before him. The skin was nearly translucent, a clear gray aspic of tissue and muscle fibers. Beneath the surface, veins and capillaries were clearly visible, pulsing slightly, blue and crimson strands threading along arms, legs, and thickening like rope at the man's neck. "This man's still *alive*. . . ."

Dr. Bronschweig shrugged. "Technically and biologically. But he'll never recover."

The Cigarette-Smoking Man shook his head. "How can this be?"

"The developing organism is using his life energy, digesting bone and tissue. We've just slowed the process." He reached to grasp the swivel neck of a lamp, redirecting it so that it shone directly on the fireman's torso. Beneath the smooth spongy planes of his chest, something moved.

The Cigarette-Smoking Man grimaced.

On the gurney, the body of the fireman shuddered. A ripple seemed to race through it, the glistening translucent skin shuddering the way a sea nettle does when it flounders upon a beach. The chest heaved gently, as though something inside had moved and stretched. A closer look revealed a hand attached to what had to be an organism.

Then the darkness *blinked.* Just once, very slowly; and resolved itself into an eye, almond-shaped, watchful.

The Cigarette-Smoking Man gazed at it, his mind working frantically as he measured all the possibilities of what was before him, all the consequences. . . .

"Do you want us to destroy this one, too?" Dr. Bronschweig was asking. "Before it gestates?"

The Cigarette-Smoking Man waited before replying. "No," he said at last. "No . . . we need to try out the vaccine on it."

"And if it's unsuccessful?"

"Burn it. Like the others."

Dr. Bronschweig frowned. "This man's family will want to see the body laid to rest."

The Cigarette-Smoking Man made a dismissive gesture. "Tell them he was trying to save the young boy's life. That he died heroically, like the other firemen."

"Of what?"

"They seemed to buy our story about the Hanta virus." The Cigarette-Smoking Man pursed his lips and stared meditatively at the figure before him, as though seeing past it to the man it had once been. "You'll make sure the families are taken care of financially, along with a sizable donation to the community."

He continued to gaze at the fireman. Finally he said, "Maybe a small roadside memorial." Then he turned, and without another word left the chamber.

CHAPTER

6

BETHESDA NAVAL HOSPITAL
BETHESDA, MARYLAND

I nside Walter Reed it smelled like any other hospital, disinfectant and chemical lemon, alcohol swabs and
air-conditioning. But the few people Mulder and Scully
passed wore navy uniforms, not standard-issue scrubs, and

the shadowy figure eating at the end of the hallway was not a nurse but a very young man in uniform, his head bent over the *Washington Post*. At the sound of their footsteps he looked up, alert as though it were not 3:30 in the morning.

"ID and floor you're visiting?" he said.

They flashed him their FBI IDs. "We're going down to the morgue," Mulder explained.

The guard shook his head. "That area is currently off limits to anyone other than authorized medical personnel."

Mulder eyed him coldly. "On whose orders?"

"General McAddie's."

Mulder didn't miss a beat. "General McAddie is who requested our coming here. We were awakened at three A.M. and told to get down here immediately."

"I don't know anything about that." The young naval guard frowned, glancing at the clipboard on his desk.

"Well, call General McAddie." Mulder stared impatiently down the corridor.

"I don't have his number."

"They can patch you in through the switchboard."

Next to Mulder, Scully stood and gazed distractedly into space. The guard bit his lip and nervously checked his watch, then picked up the phone and began flipping through a huge directory. Mulder registered outraged disbelief.

"You don't know the switchboard number?"

"I'm calling my C.O.—"

With a stabbing motion, Mulder reached over and

pressed his finger against the phone, disconnecting it. He glared at the guard.

"Listen, son, we don't have time to dick around here, watching you demonstrate your ignorance in the chain of command. The order came direct from General McAddie. Call *him*. We'll conduct our business while you confirm authorization."

Without looking back, Mulder steered Scully past the security desk. Behind them the fresh-faced young guard tentatively picked up the phone again.

"Why don't you go on ahead down, and I'll confirm authorization," he called after them.

Mulder nodded curtly. "Thank you."

They walked briskly down the corridor, only relaxing their pose when they'd turned the corner into another, more dimly lit hallway.

"Why is a morgue suddenly off limits on orders of a general?"

"Guess we'll find out," Scully replied, and pointed to the entrance to the morgue.

Inside they were met by a blast of frigid air and the dank sour odors of formaldehyde and disinfectant. In the cold room, row after row of gurneys stretched in ominous formation, each holding the familiar alpine landscape of a body beneath a white sheet. Scully made her way quickly down first one row and then another, glancing at IDs and dangling clipboards until she found what they had come here to find.

"This is one of the firemen who died in Dallas?" she asked, undoing the cat's cradle of roping that bound the still form on the gurney.

Mulder nodded. "According to this tag."

"And you're looking for?"

"Cause of death."

Scully gave him a long-suffering look. "I can tell you that without even looking at him. Concussive organ failure due to proximal exposure to source and flying debris—"

She dropped the roping and pulled out the autopsy chart that she found on the gurney. "This body has already been autopsied, Mulder," she explained patiently. "You can tell from the way it's been wrapped and dressed."

Undeterred, Mulder worked to remove the sheet from the body. The first thing they saw was that it was still clad in its fireman's uniform. One sleeve lay empty alongside the torso, and where the chest had been the uniform sank until it grazed the bottom of the gurney.

"Does this fit the description you just read me, Scully?" Mulder asked softly, as his partner circled the gurney to join him.

"Oh my god. This man's tissue—" She reached into her pocket, withdrew a pair of latex gloves, and quickly slid them on. Then she leaned and with one latex-clad finger gently palpated the man's chest. "It's—it's like *jelly*."

She moved to gingerly touch the man's face and neck, carefully unbuttoning his uniform. "There's some kind of cellular breakdown. It's completely edematous."

Her hands expertly checked for lesions, burns, anything she might normally have found on the victim of a bombing. She peeled aside the man's shirt, shaking her head. "Mulder, there's been no autopsy performed. There's no Y incision here, no internal exam."

Mulder picked up the autopsy report and shook it. "You're telling me the cause of death on this report is false. That this man *didn't* die from an explosion, or from flying debris."

She took a step back from the gurney. "I don't know *what* killed this man. I'm not sure if anybody else could claim to, either."

"I want to bring him into the lab. I'd like for you to examine him more closely, Scully."

She stared at the body, then at Mulder. After a moment she nodded. Together they pushed the gurney out of the freezer, and through the swinging doors that opened onto the pathology lab. Mulder pushed the gurney over to the wall. Scully flipped the lights on, taking in the familiar array of equipment, dissecting tools, and refrigerators for storing samples, glittering hemostats and neat stacks of freshly laundered sheets, boxes and boxes full of latex gloves, surgical masks, aprons, scrubs—all the tools of her trade. Finally she walked over to where Mulder waited alongside the gurney.

"You knew this man didn't die at the bomb site before we got here."

Mulder gave her a noncommittal look. "I'd been told as much."

"You're saying the bombing was a cover-up. Of what?"

"I don't know. But I have a hunch that what you're going to find here isn't anything that can be categorized or easily referenced."

Scully waited to hear if there was going to be more in the way of an explanation—or apology. When there wasn't, she tugged at one latex glove and sighed, shaking her head. "Mulder, this is going to take some time, and *somebody's* going to figure out soon enough that we're not even supposed to *be* here." She closed her eyes for a moment, opened them and said, "I'm in serious violation of medical ethics."

Mulder pointed at the body on the gurney. "We're being *blamed* for these deaths, Scully. I want to know what this man died of. Don't you?"

She stared at him, then back down at the body. His words hung in the air between them, something between a challenge and an entreaty. Finally she turned to the tray table set up on the wall behind them, the rows of sterilized scalpels and scissors and tweezers and knives that lay there, waiting. In silence she began gathering what she would need to do her job.

•   •   •

DUPONT CIRCLE
WASHINGTON, D.C.

Connecticut Avenue was nearly empty when Mulder crossed it, stepping up onto the sidewalk and winding between stacks of plastic garbage bags heaped onto the curb, waiting for collection. His cab pulled away behind him, joining a meager parade of vehicles: garbage truck, another Yellow Cab, police cruiser. Mulder scarcely noticed the latter, until he started down R Street and saw two other cruisers pulled up in front of a brick row house. He glanced at the address scrawled on the paper in his hand, then started up the walk. Cheerless gray light spilled onto the front stairs; the door to the row house was open. Mulder slowed his steps, hesitating at the entrance, then went inside.

It was a typical Dupont Circle apartment. A lot of money bought you a little space and a nice address, and that was about it. An unmade futon bed occupied one corner of the room; a kitchenette still held the remains of breakfast. In the main room several uniformed officers milled about, examining a stack of videotapes in black plastic slipcovers, rifling through desk drawers, peering into the disk drive of a computer. A small office had been set up in what was intended to be a bedroom. Here a police detective contemplated stacks of what appeared to be OB/GYN journals. He looked up as Mulder's shadow fell across the doorway.

"Is this Dr. Kurtzweil's residence?"

The detective eyed him suspiciously. "You got some kind of business with him?"

"I'm looking for him." Mulder's tone was noncommittal.

"Looking for him for what?"

Mulder pulled out his ID and flashed it at him. The detective glanced at it, then looked up and called to his partners in the next room, "Hey, the Feds are looking for him, too." He turned back to Mulder. "Real nice business he's got, huh?"

Mulder frowned slightly. "What's that?"

"Selling naked pictures of little kids over his computer."

Mulder nodded, trying not to show his surprise. He stepped into the middle of the small office, staring at the bookshelf by the detective. On each lurid dust jacket the same name appeared in big, gold-embossed letters.

DR. ALVIN KURTZWEIL

Mulder slipped alongside the detective and withdrew one of the books. Surprisingly light for such a big volume—five hundred pages, at least—printed on cheap paper that was already yellowing. He flipped through it, then read the cover.

THE FOUR HORSEMAN OF THE GLOBAL DOMINATION CONSPIRACY

Mulder glanced over as the detective appeared at his elbow. "You looking for him for some other reason?"

"Yeah." He replaced the book and gazed at the detective through narrowed eyes. "I had an appointment for a pelvic examination."

The detective and other policemen stared at him with undisguised repugnance. When Mulder smiled they suddenly broke into raucous laughter.

"You want a call if we turn up Kurtzweil?"

Mulder turned and started back for the door. "No. Don't bother."

Outside the sky had its customary livid, near-dawn glow: yellow crime lights, lavender exhaust, the city's inescapable humidity all conspiring to give the landscape a bruised look. Mulder exited the apartment building, hoping it wouldn't take too long to find a cab, then he noticed a lanky silhouette gesturing furtively at him a few yards away. Mulder looked over his shoulder, then back at the figure. It was Kurtzweil, standing with obvious unease in front of a narrow gap between two row houses. When he saw that Mulder had noticed him he nodded, then stepped back and disappeared into the darkness. Mulder hurried after him.

He found Kurtzweil halfway down a dank alley that smelled of urine and spilled beer. Broken bottles and crack vials crunched underfoot—not Dupont Circle looking its best. Kurtzweil huddled up against the brick wall and shook his head furiously.

"See this bullshit?" he said contemptuously. "Cloak and dagger stuff . . . Somebody knows I'm talking to you."

Mulder shrugged. "Not according to the men in blue."

"What is it this time? Kiddie porn again? Sexual battery of a patient?" Kurtzweil spat. "I've had my license taken away in three states."

Mulder nodded. "They want to discredit you—for what?"

"For what?" Kurtzweil threw his head back and stared at the liverish sky far overhead. "Because I'm a dangerous man! Because I know too much about the truth . . ."

"You mean that end-of-the-world, apocalyptic garbage you write?"

A spark flared in Kurtzweil's eyes. "You know my work?" he asked hopefully.

Mulder took a deep breath. "Dr. Kurtzweil, I'm not interested in bigoted ideas about race or genocide. I don't believe in the Elders of Zion, the Knights Templar, the Bilderburg Group, *or* in a one-world Jew-run government—"

Kurtzweil grinned. "I don't either, but it sure sells books."

Disgusted, Mulder spun on his heel and headed out. Before he reached the sidewalk Kurtzweil collared him.

"I was right about Dallas, wasn't I, Agent Mulder?"

Mulder sighed and stared at him. "How?" he demanded.

"I picked up the historical document of the venality and hypocrisy of the American government. The daily newspaper."

Impatience flickered across Mulder's face. "You said the firemen and the boy were found in the temporary offices of the Federal Emergency Management Agency. Why?"

Kurtzweil pulled his raincoat tight about his chest and glanced nervously down the alley. "According to the newspaper, FEMA had been called out to manage an outbreak of the Hanta virus. Are you familiar with the Hanta virus, Agent Mulder?"

"It was a deadly virus spread by deer mice in the Southwest U.S. several years ago."

"And are you familiar with FEMA? What the Federal Emergency Management Agency's *real* power is?"

Mulder raised his eyebrows, waiting to hear how this was all going to fit. Kurtzweil went on quickly, "FEMA allows the White House to suspend constitutional government upon declaration of a national emergency. It allows the creation of a non-elected government. Think about that, Agent Mulder."

Mulder thought. Kurtzweil's voice rose slightly, knowing he finally had an audience. "What is an agency with such broad sweeping power doing managing a small viral outbreak in suburban Texas?"

"Are you saying," Mulder said slowly, "that it *wasn't* a small outbreak?"

Kurtzweil's expression looked positively feverish. "I'm saying it wasn't the Hanta virus."

From the street came the sudden *yowp* of a siren. The two men started, then backed more tightly against the damp brick walls as a police car cruised slowly down the street. When it was gone, Mulder hissed, "What *was* it?"

Kurtzweil stared at his hands, finally said, "When we were young men in the military, your father and I were recruited for a project. They told us it was biological warfare. A virus. There were . . . rumors . . . about its origins."

Mulder shook his head impatiently. "What killed those men?"

"What killed them I won't even write about," Kurtzweil exploded. "I tell you, they'd do more than just harass me. They have the future to protect."

Mulder regarded him coolly. "I'll know soon enough."

But Kurtzweil was too worked up to hear him. "What killed those men can't be identified in simple medical terms," he went on heatedly. "My god, we can't even wrap our minds around something as obvious as HIV! We have no *context* for what killed those men, or any appreciation of the scale in which it will be unleashed in the future. Of how it will be transmitted, of the environmental factors involved . . ."

"A plague?"

"The plague to end all plagues, Agent Mulder," whispered Kurtzweil. "A silent weapon for a quiet war. The systematic release of an indiscriminate organism for which the men who bring it on still have no cure. They've been working on this for *fifty years*—" He punched the air for emphasis. "—while the rest of the world was fighting gooks and commies, these men have been secretly negotiating a planned Armageddon."

Mulder frowned. "Negotiating with *whom?*"

"I think you know." Kurtzweil's mouth grew tight. "The timetable has been set. It will happen on a holiday, when people are away from their homes. When our elected officials are at their resorts or out of the country. The President will declare a state of emergency, at which time all federal agencies, *all* government, will come under the power of the Federal Emergency Management Agency.

"FEMA, Agent Mulder. The secret government."

Mulder whistled. "And they tell me *I'm* paranoid."

Kurtzweil shook his head fiercely. "Something's gone wrong—something unanticipated. Go back to Dallas and dig, Agent Mulder. Or we're only going to find out like the rest of the country—when it's too late."

The older man shoved his hands into his pockets, turned, and walked quickly down the alley. Mulder stared after him, torn between annoyance, disbelief, and his own suspicions that Kurtzweil might well be on to something. Finally he called, "How can I reach you?"

"You can't," Kurtzweil replied without looking back. Mulder ran to catch up with him, pulling out his cell phone.

"Here—" he said breathlessly. Kurtzweil halted and stared at him. His eyes were wide, and for the first time Mulder recognized in the doctor's face that blend of fanaticism and fear that marked true and intense paranoia. He forced the cell phone into Kurtzweil's hand, then shook a finger at him.

"No calling Hawaii."

Mulder made his way in silence back to the leaden expanse of Connecticut Avenue.

●   ●   ●

BETHESDA NAVAL HOSPITAL
BETHESDA, MARYLAND

Dana Scully was so involved with her autopsy of the fireman that she almost didn't hear the brisk tread in the hallway and, moments later, the ominous click of a door opening. She whipped around, eyes wide above her surgical mask. Vague figures moved behind a frosted glass window: she recognized the young guard she and Mulder had scammed in the hallway, and two others wearing the uniform of military police. Without a sound she yanked the sheet back over the fireman's corpse, then darted across the laboratory to the freezer door.

She opened it as quickly and quietly as she could, slipped inside the frigid room, and shut the heavy metal door behind her. She winced as it clicked shut. Faint voices rose in the next room and she tensed, holding her breath as she tried to hear what they were saying.

". . . *said they had clearance from General McAddie* . . ."

Abruptly the cloistered quiet of the freezer was broken by the chirping of her cell phone. Scully patted frantically at her coat, trying to silence it before it rang again. Before it could ring a second time she palmed the phone and hit the ON button.

"Scully . . . ?"

She crouched behind the door, her breathing quick and shallow, terrified that the guard was about to burst in. Mulder's voice came again from the phone. "Scully?"

She drew it slowly to her face. "Yeah," she said in a hoarse whisper.

"Why are you whispering?" Behind him she could hear the sounds of intermittent traffic, the bleat of a passing radio; he was at a pay phone.

"I can't really talk right now," she said, staring up at the door.

"What did you find?"

She took a breath. "Evidence of a massive infection."

"What kind of infection."

"I don't know."

Near silence in which she could hear static, the roar of a bus. Finally Mulder said, "Scully. Listen to me. I'm going home, then I'm booking a flight to Dallas. I'm getting you a ticket, too."

"*Mulder*—"

"I need you there with me," he went on quickly, not giving her the chance to argue. "I need your expertise on this. The bomb we found was meant to destroy those bodies and whatever they were infected by."

She shook her head. "I've got a hearing tomorrow—"

"I'll have you back for it, Scully, I promise. Maybe with evidence that could blow your hearing away."

"Mulder, I can't," Scully's voice rose. She bit her lip, angry and fearful of discovery. "I'm already *way* past the point of common sense here—"

Sudden voices sounded from the other side of the door. Without a "good-bye," Scully punched the phone off and shoved it into a pocket. Then she slid across the floor, ducking beneath one of the gurneys. She pressed herself back as far as she could go and held her breath as the door to the freezer opened.

Footsteps. From where she was hidden Scully could see the guard's carefully buffed regulation-issue shoes pass within inches of her face. Two other pairs of feet followed, as the MPs crossed the freezer room, their steps echoing loudly on the linoleum floor. It was cold enough that Scully's entire body began to shake. She gritted her teeth, the gurney's metal shelf pressing against her back like a blade.

At the far wall the MPs hesitated. Scully watched as first one and then another stood on tiptoe. There was the bang of a steel cabinet being opened and closed; then the MPs turned and went back to the door, the naval guard behind them. He had just passed the gurney where she huddled when abruptly he stopped. Scully held her breath, heart pounding; she could have grabbed him by the ankle if she wanted to.

Go, she thought, and closed her eyes. Go, *leave, just go* . . .

They left. The freezer's heavy doors slammed shut. Scully sighed, and waited until it was safe to follow.

CHAPTER 7

FORENSICS LABORATORY
FBI FIELD OFFICE
DALLAS, TEXAS

"Y ou're looking for what amounts to a needle in a haystack." The field agent waved his hand to indicate the room around them, an open space the size of a basketball court. "I'm afraid the explosion was so devastating there hasn't been whole lot we've been able to put together just yet."

Mulder had to agree. There were stacks of debris, twisted girders, roped-off areas where forensics experts sat and painstakingly tried to piece together what had been an office, or a kitchen, or a doorway. It looked like the most tedious job in the world. Mulder stopped and stared at a table covered with what resembled a thousand scattered silvery blobs of solder. He raised an eyebrow, then turned back to the field agent.

"I'm looking for anything out of the ordinary. Maybe something from the FEMA offices where the bodies were found."

The field agent nodded, passing Mulder and pointing to another table. "We weren't expecting to find those remains, of course. They went right off to Washington."

Mulder looked away, hoping his frustration and disappointment wouldn't show. "Was there anything in those offices that didn't go to D.C.?"

The field agent gestured at the table. The jumbled contents looked as if they'd been there for months. There were dusty glass bottles filled with what looked like metal screws and nails. Strewn across the table were a number of brushes of varying shapes and sizes, as well as tweezers, microscopes, and a very large magnifying glass.

"Some bone fragments came up in the sift this morning." The field agent picked up one of the bottles and gazed at its contents. "We thought there'd been another fatality, but then we found out that FEMA had recovered them from an archaeological site out of town."

"Have you examined them?"

"No." The field agent shrugged and replaced the bottle. "Just fossils, as far as we know."

Mulder nodded, when a figure standing in the doorway caught his eye. He lifted his chin very slightly and said, "I'd like this person to take a look, if you don't mind."

At the entrance to the workroom, Scully stood with arms crossed and stared at Mulder. Before he could call out to her, she walked across the room to join them. The field agent acknowledged her with a nod of greeting.

"Let me just see if I can lay my hands on what you're looking for," he said, and headed off into the maze of detritus behind them.

Mulder leaned against the table and gave Scully the once-over, twice. "You said you weren't coming."

"I wasn't planning on it," she said coolly. "Particularly after spending a half hour in cold storage this morning. But I got a better look at the blood and tissue samples I took from the fireman."

Mulder straightened. "What did you find?"

Scully lowered her voice. "Something I couldn't show to anyone else. Not without more information. And not without causing the kind of attention I'd just as soon avoid right now."

She took a deep breath, and said, "The virus those men were infected with contains a protein code I've never seen before. What it did to them, it did extremely fast. And unlike the AIDS virus or any other aggressive strain, it survives very nicely *outside* the body."

Mulder's voice was a near whisper. "How was it contracted?"

"That I don't know. But if it's through simple contact or blood to blood, and if it doesn't respond to conventional treatments, it could be a serious health threat."

Mulder started to reply excitedly, but at that moment the field agent reappeared. In his hands he carried a wooden tray holding several cork-topped glass vials. "Like I said, these are fossils," he announced, setting the tray down. "And they weren't near the blast center, so they aren't going to help you much."

"May I?" Scully waited for the field agent's nod, then picked up the tray. One by one she held the vials up to the light. They held bone fragments, the shattered remains of tibia and jaws and teeth. She selected one vial and stepped over to the chair beside a microscope, sat, and very carefully tapped out a tiny fragment onto the viewing bed. She leaned forward, adjusting the focus until the fossilized sliver came into view.

Almost immediately she looked back up at Mulder. He took in her expression and quickly turned to the field agent. "You said you knew the location of the archaeological site where these were found?"

The agent nodded agreeably. "Show you right on a map," he drawled. "C'mon."

•   •   •

BLACKWOOD, TEXAS

The midday sun beat down upon raw red earth and dead grass, the domed white tents rising like huge, dust-stained eggs amid the unmanned trucks surrounding them. Several large generators gave forth a muted hum, but otherwise the scene was unutterably desolate. And strange.

Within the central tent, things were busier but no less strange. At the edge of an earthen hole, a small bulldozer wrestled with a large Lucite container set into its shovel, maneuvering it until it was a few yards from the opening. Monitors and gauges covered every inch of the container's surface, along with oxygen tanks and something resembling a circulating refrigeration unit. It looked more like the sort of thing you'd find on a lunar landing module than in the Texas flatlands, and that's exactly what it was: a self-contained life-support system, its interior glazed with a thin, sugary layer of frost.

The bulldozer's engine cut off. Several technicians appeared. They lined up alongside the machine's shovel and lifted off the container, carrying it gingerly toward the hole. As they did so, a flap at the end of the room opened and Dr. Bronschweig appeared, clad in his Haz-Mat suit, hood unzipped so that it hung across his shoulders. He waved curtly at the technicians and started down the ladder leading into the hole.

"I need to have those settings checked and reset," he

called, pointing at the gauge-ridden container. "I need a *steady* minus two Celsius though the transfer of the body, after I administer the vaccine. Got that? *Minus two.*"

The technicians nodded. They set the container down and began checking gauges. Bronschweig pulled his hood on and disappeared down the hole, bumping against the clear hatch as he went.

Below, in the ice cave, it was dark save for the arctic blue glow coming from the plastic-draped area at one end of the chamber. Refrigeration vents continued to pump freezing air into the dim space. Dr. Bronschweig moved stiffly across the cave, halting at the entrance to the eerily glowing alcove. With one gloved hand he moved aside the plastic drapery and entered.

Behind him plastic crinkled as the sheeting fell back into place. He stepped over to the gurney beneath its rack of monitors. A clear plastic bubble covered it, encasing the body of the fireman. Dr. Bronschweig fished in his pocket and withdrew a syringe and ampule. He reached for a work light, moving it until its steady bright beam fell on the litter, and leaned closer to open the plastic casing. What he saw there made him gasp.

The body looked as though it had exploded. Where the inner organs had been, there was only an empty cavity, as though whatever had been inside had devoured them. The gurney's plastic casing was smeared with crimson and the remains of gnawed bone and tissue.

Sheer panic got him to the base of the ladder mere seconds later. "It's gone!" he shouted, his voice muffled by his hood. Frantically he worked at the snaps and zippers, and yanked it off. *"It's gone!"*

"It's *what?*"

Overhead, the face of one of the technicians appeared, framed by the life-support cannister behind him.

"It's left the body," Dr. Bronschweig cried breathlessly. Other technicians crowded around the first, as Bronschweig began climbing up the ladder. "I think it's gestated."

He froze, squinting into the darkness below him. "Wait," he said in a hoarse whisper. "I see it—"

In the shadows, something moved. Bronschweig held his breath, waiting. A moment later it appeared. Limned in blue light from the corner, the plastic rustling as it parted and the creature came through. It moved tentatively, almost timidly, like something newly born.

"Jesus Lord," whispered Bronschweig. His eyes widened in nervous wonder as he stared. Then, after a minute had passed, he took a gentle step back down to the ground. "So much for little green men . . ."

"You see it?" a technician called anxiously.

"Yeah. It's . . . amazing." He looked up at the faces ringed around the entrance to the cavern. "You want to get down here—"

Shakily he began working at the ampule, trying to fit it onto the syringe and the plunger in place. He glanced back at the shadows where the creature was, and—

It was gone. With deathly slowness Bronschweig

turned, fearfully scanning the cavern for where it might have fled. There was nothing.

His hand tightened on the syringe as though it were a pistol, and then he saw it in the shadows across the cave. He stared at it for a split second, paralyzed, as its hands lifted and long pointed claws extended. With inhuman ferocity it lunged at him.

Screaming, he stabbed out with the syringe, managing to inject some of the precious fluid before the thing threw him across the length of the cave. Terrified, Bronschweig staggered to his feet and made his way to the foot of the ladder. Blood trickled from a wound at his neck, but most of the damage seemed to have come to his suit, which flapped around him like a tattered sail.

"Hey," he cried brokenly, staring up the ladder into the technicians' stunned faces. "I need help. . . ."

He glanced behind him, searching warily for signs of the creature, then back up the ladder. "HEY—What are you doing?"

They were closing the hatch. Shoving it down as fast as they could and frantically screwing the locks into place, even as Bronschweig watched in disbelief. He flung himself up the ladder, heedless of pain or the blood blossoming across his white suit. He screamed, but his screams went unheard. Above him there was a dull roar, and a dark blur floated across the transparent hatch. The bulldozer's shovel rose and fell like a striking hand, and with each blow dumped another load of earth onto the hatch. They were burying him alive.

In stunned silence he stood there, unmoving, unable to think, when from behind him there came a muffled sound. And it was on him, pulling him down, pulling him off the ladder, and down into the darkness of the cave.

CHAPTER 8

SOMERSET, ENGLAND

A man stood at the conservatory window of a mansion, looking down as his grandchildren romped and raced, laughing breathlessly, across an impeccably manicured lawn. This was one of the few things that gave him anything like peace: sunset, and the sound of grandchildren laughing.

"Sir?"

Behind him came the voice of his valet. The Well-Manicured Man continued to stare out the window, smiling.

"Sir, you have a call."

He turned to see his valet holding open the conservatory door. For a moment the Well-Manicured Man remained, gazing wistfully at the idyllic vista below. Finally he headed toward his study.

The twilight seemed deeper here, lavender shadows darkening to violet where bookcases mounted from floor to ceiling and all the trappings of wealth lay accumulated and forgotten in the corners and on the walls. The Well-Manicured Man ignored all of these, striding to a desk by the window where a telephone blinked insistently. He picked it up, positioning himself so that he could continue to look down upon his grandchildren playing tag.

"Yes," he said.

From the other end of the line came a familiar voice, smoke-strained, laconic. "We have a situation. The members are assembling."

The Well-Manicured Man winced; he did not like surprises. "Is it an emergency?"

"Yes. A meeting is set, tonight in London. We must determine a course."

The Well-Manicured Man's face tightened. "Who called this meeting?"

"Strughold." At the sound of this name, the Well-

Manicured Man nodded grimly. There could be no further questions. The voice on the phone continued. "He's just gotten on a plane in Tunis."

Without replying, the Well-Manicured Man dropped the phone back into its cradle. A child was screaming. He rushed to the window.

On the lawn beneath him, the lovely tableau had been shattered. From the house people were running—his valet, the housekeeper, the gardening staff—to where the children had gathered. A boy, his youngest grandchild. He lay on his side, his face contorted and white as paper. One leg was awkwardly crumpled under him. The valet reached him first and knelt beside him, gently stroking the boy's forehead and calling out orders to the watching staff. As the valet tenderly lifted the child into his arms, the Well-Manicured Man raced from the study, all thoughts of Strughold momentarily banished.

He did not arrive in Kensington until shortly after eight that night. The chauffeured town car slipped silently into the circular drive and stopped before the front door of a large but unpretentious red-brick building, its front door bearing neither name nor number.

"Has Strughold arrived?" the Well-Manicured Man asked the valet who had met his car.

The other man indicated a long, dimly lit hallway. "They're waiting in the library, sir."

He led the Well-Manicured Man down the hall. The faintest susurrus of voices rose as they approached the library, where the valet inclined his head and left him. Inside, walnut paneling and discreet touches of brass and silver ornamented a large room where a group of men stood, staring at the steely blue eye of a TV monitor. A poor quality black-and-white video was playing, dark forms moving jerkily across a darker background dotted with electrical snow. As he entered, the men turned expectantly.

The Well-Manicured Man surveyed the group before joining them. A dozen men of his own age and rank, though none possessed his effortless hauteur. Faces no one would recognize, though a word from one of them might bring a government crashing to its knees. Men who remained in the shadows.

In the center of the group stood a small, lean man with close-cropped hair, at once elegant and imposing. His gaze met the newcomer's, holding it for a moment too long, and the Well-Manicured Man felt the slightest *frisson* of unease.

"We began to worry," Strughold said in the deceptively gentle tone one might use to scold a beloved child. "Some of us have traveled so far, and you are the last to arrive."

"I'm sorry." The Well-Manicured Man tilted his head in deference to Strughold. "My grandson fell and broke his leg." It was all the apology he would offer, even to Strughold.

"What's down there, Stevie? Anything? "

"Stevie? You okay?"

"Scully, listen to me."

"You've got about fourteen minutes to get
this building evacuated."

"We're under pressure to give an accurate picture of what
happened in the Dallas explosion to the Attorney General."

"If they want someone to blame, they can blame me. Agent Scully doesn't deserve this."

"I think that just about does it, Spooky."

"It's left the body. I think it's gestated—"

"This is weird, Mulder. Any thoughts on why anybody would be growing corn in the middle of the desert?"

"Not unless those are giant Jiffy Pop poppers out there."

"You found something?"
"Yes. On the Texas border. Some kind of experiment."

"Find Agent Scully."

"Only then will you realize the scope and grandeur of The Project."

"Breathe!"

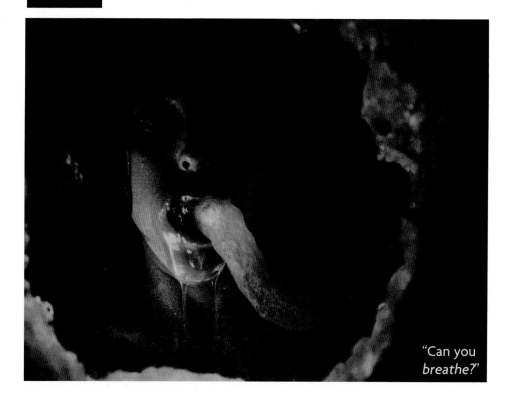

"Can you *breathe?*"

"Come on . . . it's time to go."

"One man alone cannot fight the future. "

The other man seemed not to have heard him at all. Instead he went on smoothly, "While we've been made to wait, we've watched surveillance tapes which have raised more concerns."

"More concerns than what?" he asked, frowning.

"We've been forced to reassess our role in Colonization." Strughold's tone was even; he might have been discussing a minor unpleasantness on the trading floor. "Some new facts of biology have presented themselves."

"The virus has mutated," another voice broke in, more urgently.

The Well-Manicured Man looked taken aback. "On its own?"

"We don't know." The Cigarette-Smoking Man withdrew his lighter. "So far, there's only the isolated case in Dallas."

"Its effect on the host has changed," said Strughold. "The virus no longer just invades the brain as a controlling organism. It's developed a way to modify the host body."

The Well-Manicured Man's mouth grew taut. "Into what?"

"A new extraterrestrial biological entity."

A moment while the men took this in. The Well-Manicured Man stared at Strughold in disbelief. "My god . . ."

Strughold nodded. "The geometry of mass infection presents certain conceptual reevaluations for us. About our place in their Colonization . . ."

"This isn't about Colonization!" the Well-Manicured Man exploded. "It's spontaneous repopulation! All our work . . ."

His voice trailed off, and he turned to gaze at the men around him. "If it's true, then they've been using us all along. We've been laboring under a lie!"

"It could be an isolated case," one of the others offered.

"How can we *know*?"

Strughold's voice rang out calmly as others joined in. "We're going to tell them what we've found. What we've learned. By turning over a body infected with the gestating organism."

"In hope of *what*? Learning that it's true?" The Well-Manicured Man stared furiously at Strughold. "That we are nothing more than digestives for the creation of a new race of alien life forms!"

"Let me remind you who is the new race. And who is the old," Strughold responded coolly. "What would be gained by withholding anything from them? By pretending ignorance? If this signals that Colonization has already begun, then our knowledge may forestall it."

"And if it doesn't?" retorted the Well-Manicured Man. "By cooperating now we're but beggars to our own demise! Our ignorance lay in cooperating with the Colonists at all."

Strughold shrugged. "Cooperation is our only chance of saving ourselves."

Beside him the Cigarette-Smoking Man nodded. "They still need us to carry out their preparations."

"We'll continue to use them as they do us," said Strughold. "If only to play for more time. To continue work on our vaccine."

"Our vaccine may have no effect!" cried the Well-Manicured Man.

"Well, without a cure for the virus, we're nothing more than digestives anyway."

All eyes turned to see how the Well-Manicured Man would react to this. He was well respected by the members of the Syndicate. If his was now the lone voice crying in the wilderness, they would still hear him out.

"My lateness might as well have been absence," he said in barely restrained fury. "A course has already been taken."

Strughold gestured at the TV and the Cigarette-Smoking Man pointed a remote at the monitor. The tape froze. The Well-Manicured Man glanced at the screen to see a hospital corridor, where Mulder and Scully were talking with a young naval guard. "There are complications."

"Do they know?"

"Mulder was in Dallas when we were trying to destroy the evidence," said the Cigarette-Smoking Man. "He's gone back again now. Someone has tipped him off."

"Who?"

"Kurtzweil, we think."

"We've allowed this man his freedoms," interrupted Strughold. "His books have actually helped us to facilitate plausible denial. Has he outlived his usefulness to us?"

"No one believes Kurtzweil or his books," said the Well-

Manicured Man impatiently. "He's toiler. A crank."

"Mulder believes him," someone else said.

"Then Kurtzweil must be removed," said the Cigarette-Smoking Man.

"As must Mulder," pronounced Strughold.

The Well-Manicured Man shook his head angrily. "Kill Mulder and we risk turning one man's quest into a crusade."

Strughold turned on him with a look of icy malevolence. "We've discredited Agent Mulder. Taken away his reputation. Who mourns the death of a broken man?"

The Well-Manicured Man met his gaze with one of challenging disdain. "Mulder is far from broken."

"Then you must taken away what he holds most valuable," said Strughold. He turned to stare at the monitor, where a woman's face now took up most of the screen. "The one thing in the world that he can't live without."

CHAPTER 9

BLACKWOOD, TEXAS

"I don't know, Mulder . . ." Scully shook her head, squinting into the glaring sunlight. In front of her a children's playground rose from the otherwise barren earth, cheerful counterpoint to the surrounding Texas desolation. "He didn't mention a *park*."

95

Mulder paced from the swings to the jungle gym to the slide. Everything brand-spanking new, plastic and painted metal in bright primary colors: blue, red, purple, yellow. The grass underfoot seemed newly minted as well, thick green grass that breathed a sweet cool scent wherever he stepped.

"This is where he marked on the geological survey map, Scully." He jabbed at the folded paper in his hand. "Where he said those fossils were unearthed."

Scully made a helpless gesture. "I don't see any evidence of an archaeological dig, or any other kind of site. Not even a sewer or a storm drain."

Mulder scanned the area, confounded. In the distance the Dallas skyline shimmered in the heat, and children rode bikes in front of a modest housing development. He went back over to Scully, and together they walked around the edges of the playground.

"You're sure the fossils you looked at showed the same signs of deterioration you saw in the fireman's body in the morgue?"

Scully nodded. "The bone was porous, as if the virus or the causative microbe were decomposing it."

"And you've never seen anything like that?"

"No." Now it was her turn to look confounded. "It didn't show up on any of the immunohistochemical tests—"

Mulder listened, staring down at his feet. Suddenly he stooped and ran his hand lightly over the tips of bright green there.

"This look like new grass to you?" he asked.

Scully tipped her head. "It looks pretty green for this climate."

Mulder knelt and dug his fingers into the thick carpet of turf. After a minute, he lifted up a corner of a new square of grass, revealing white root mass with chocolate-brown earth clinging to it. Under this the hard-baked surface of Texas dirt could be seen, brick-red and tough as sandstone.

"Ground's dry about an inch down," Mulder announced. "Somebody just laid this down. Very recently, I'd say."

Scully turned in a slow circle, looking at the brightly painted swings and seesaws. "All the equipment is brand new."

"But there's no irrigation system. Some-body's covering their tracks."

From behind them came a sound well-known from childhood, the whizzing of bikes on blacktop. Scully and Mulder turned, gazing back at the cul-de-sac where their rental car was parked near the development. Four boys were riding there. When Mulder whistled loudly at them, they stopped, puzzled, and stared blankly at him across the distance.

"Hey," called Mulder. They said nothing, only stared and shielded their eyes from the sun as the two grown-ups approached.

"Do you live around here?" asked Scully.

The boys exchanged looks. Finally one of them shrugged and said, "Yeah."

Mulder stopped and regarded them. Pretty standard-issue middle America boys in buzzcuts and T-shirts. Two of them straddled brand-new BMX bikes. "You see anybody digging around here?"

The boys remained silent, until one of them replied sullenly, "Not supposed to talk about it."

"You're not supposed to talk about it?" Scully prodded him gently. "Who told you that?"

The third boy piped up. "Nobody."

"Nobody, huh? The same Nobody who put this park in? All that nice new equipment . . ."

Mulder gestured at the swing sets, then looked sternly down into the boys' guilty faces. "They buy you those bikes, too?"

The boys shifted uncomfortably. "I think you better tell us," said Scully.

"We don't even know you," the first boy sniffed.

"Well, we're FBI agents."

The boy looked at Scully disdainfully. "*You're* not FBI agents."

Mulder suppressed a smile. "How do you know?"

"You look like door-to-door salesmen."

Mulder and Scully pulled out their badges. The boys' mouths dropped.

"They all left twenty minutes ago," one of the boys said quickly. "Going that way—"

They all pointed in the same direction.

"Thanks, guys," Mulder called. He pulled Scully after him and hurried toward the car.

The boys stood, silent, and watched as their rental car spun out onto the highway, red dust billowing behind it like smoke.

Mulder hunched at the wheel, foot to the floor. The car raced on, passing few other vehicles. Beside him Scully pored over the map, now and then looking out the window in concern.

"Unmarked tanker trucks . . ." Mulder said as to himself. "What are archaeologists hauling out in tanker trucks?"

"I don't know, Mulder."

"And where are they *going* with it?"

"That's the first question to answer, if we're going to find them."

They drove on, the sun moving slowly across the endless sky until it hung, a crimson disc, just above the horizon before them. It had been an hour since they'd seen another car. Mulder eased his foot from the accelerator, and let the car roll to stop. In front of them was an intersection. Each road seemed to go absolutely nowhere: Nowhere North or Nowhere South.

For several minutes the car sat idling. Finally Mulder spoke, rubbing his eyes.

"What are my choices?"

Scully blinked in the westerly light, then grimaced. "About a hundred miles of nothing in each direction."

"Where would they be going?"

Scully looked out her window, to where the asphalt road angled off and disappeared into the twilight. "We've got two choices. One of them wrong."

Mulder stared out his window. "You think they went left?"

Scully shook her head, her gaze unmoving. "I don't know why—I think they went right."

A few more minutes of silence passed. Then Mulder pounded his foot on the gas. The car arrowed straight ahead, onto the unpaved dirt road. They bumped over rocks and gullies, dust flaring up all around them as Mulder drove, his expression unrelentingly determined. Scully stared at him, waiting for an explanation, but he refused to meet her gaze.

Ahead of them the sun disappeared. Red and black clouds streaked the darkening sky, and a few stars pricked into view. Scully rolled down her window and breathed in the night: mesquite, sage, dust. Twenty minutes had passed, when Mulder turned to her and finally spoke.

"Five years together," he said in a tone that brooked no arguing. "How many times have I been wrong?"

A few quiet seconds pass. "At least not about driving."

Scully stared out at the night, and said nothing.

•   •   •

Hours went by. Mulder drove quickly, the silence unbroken save by the occasional wail of a dog or coyote, the shrieking of an owl. Outside the night sky glittered, nothing but stars as far as you could see, nothing at all. When the car began to slow Scully felt as though she were being awakened from a dream, and turned reluctantly from her window to gaze at what was before them.

Clouds of dust rose and settled in the velvety darkness. A few feet in front of the car, a line of fence posts stretched endlessly to the left and right, looped together by heavy strands of rusted barbed wire. Wild white roses choked the fence with briars, and prickly pear cacti were clumped everywhere. There was no gate, and as far as Scully could see, no break in the fence.

She opened the door and got out. After the car's air-conditioning, the hot Texas wind was like standing in front of a wood stove. In the distance a dog barked. Scully walked to where the headlights washed over the fence, and stared at a sign nailed to a post. Behind her, Mulder's door opened, and he stepped out to join her.

"Hey, I was right about the bomb, wasn't I?" he asked plaintively.

"This is great," said Scully. "This is fitting."

She cocked her thumb at the sign.

SOME HAVE TRIED, SOME HAVE DIED.
TURN BACK—NO TRESPASSING

"What?" demanded Mulder.

"I've got to be in Washington, D.C. in eleven hours for a hearing—the outcome of which might possibly affect one of the biggest decisions of my life. And here I am standing out in the middle of Nowhere, Texas, *chasing phantom tanker trucks.*"

"We're not chasing trucks," Mulder said hotly, "we're chasing *evidence.*"

"Of *what*, exactly?"

"That bomb in Dallas was *allowed* to go off, to hide bodies infected with a virus. A virus you detected yourself, Scully."

"They haul gas in tanker trucks, they haul oil in tanker trucks—they don't haul *viruses* in tanker trucks."

Mulder stared obstinately into the darkness. "Yeah, well, they may in this one."

"What do you mean by that?" For the first time Scully stared directly at him, her face clouded with anger and a growing suspicion. "What are you not telling me here?"

"This virus–" He turned away from her, afraid to go on.

"*Mulder*—"

"It may be extraterrestrial."

A moment while Scully gazed at him in disbelief. Then, "I don't believe this!" she exploded. "You know, I've *been* here—I've been here one too many times with you, Mulder."

He kicked at a stone and looked at her, all innocence. "Been where?"

"Pounding down some dirt road in the middle of the

night! Chasing some elusive truth on a dim hope, only to find myself *right* where I am right now, at *another* dead end—"

Her voice was abruptly cut off by the clanging of a bell. Blinding light strobed across their faces. Stunned, they whirled to stare at the barbed-wire fence.

In the sudden burst of light, a railroad crossing sign appeared to hang in the empty air. No swinging metal arms or gate, just that sign, an eerie warning in the wilderness. Mulder and Scully stared at it open-mouthed, then turned to gaze at a light burgeoning upon the horizon. As they watched, it grew larger and larger, until it resolved into the headlamp of a train speeding toward them.

Wordlessly they backed to their car, but stopped as the train rushed past. And saw then what they had been chasing through the wasteland: two unmarked white tanker trucks, loaded piggyback on the flatbed cars. In seconds it was gone, swallowed by the night. The railroad crossing sign faded into the darkness, and silence once again overtook the prairie.

As one, Mulder and Scully dashed madly back into their car. Headlights sliced through the darkness as Mulder swung the car into a hard turn, and the engine roared as they took off after the train.

They followed it for a long time, the rails glowing faintly in the headlights as they arrowed straight into the night. Around them the countryside began to change, prairie gradually giving way to higher ground, stone-covered hillocks and shallow canyons covered with dense underbrush. In the distance mountains loomed dead-black against a sky starting to fade to dawn. Foothills rose around them, choked with low-growing juniper and devil's-head cactus; except for the twin lines of the rails, there was no sign that any human had ever set foot here.

Then, very slowly, the tracks began to follow a long sloping upward grade. The belly of the rental car scraped against rocks, the wheels jounced in and out of foot-high ruts; and still they drove on, chugging uphill. Until, at last, they could go no farther; the railroad tracks disappeared into the mountain, with not the slightest hint of what might lie on the other side of the tunnel. The car swung across the rails, tires spinning on the gravel bed, and came to a stop at the edge of a gorge. Scully and Mulder clambered out, pulling on their jackets against the chill bite of desert air. In the near distance, beyond the gorge on the other side of the mountain, a strange opalescent glow stained the air.

"What do you think it is?" Scully asked in a low voice.

Mulder jammed his hands in his pockets and shook his head. "I have no idea."

They started toward it, stumbling as they climbed down the rough hillside. Before them a great plateau stretched as far as they could see, and at the edge of this rose what was illuminating the night: two gigantic, glowing white domes that seemed to float in the darkness. Rolling to a stop beside them was the train that bore the unmarked tanker trucks.

Mulder pointed. Scully nodded, and without speaking they continued down, sliding through loose scree and grabbing onto dried shrubs to keep from falling. Finally they reached bottom. Ahead of them stretched the high desert plateau. They moved more quickly now, just short of running as they made their way across the waste. In the near distance something shimmered and rustled in the cold wind, and there was a grassy odor. But it wasn't until they were nearly upon it that the eerie glow from the domes revealed what lay before them.

"*Look,*" breathed Scully in disbelief.

In the half light stretched acres and acres of cornfields, as incongruous in that desert as fresh water or snow-capped hills. Wind rippled through the stalks, corn tassels whispered; and Mulder and Scully walked slowly until they stood at the very edge of the field.

They entered the field, walking one behind the other down a row lined with stalks that grew two or three feet above their heads. Scully shook her head. "This is weird, Mulder."

"Very weird." He gazed to where the twin domes rose cloudlike above the distant edge of the field.

"Any thoughts on why anybody'd be growing corn in the middle of the desert?"

Mulder flicked a fallen husk from his shoulder and pointed at the domes. "Not unless those are giant Jiffy Pop poppers out there."

They went on, the wind rattling the stalks as they

passed row after row of corn like some landscape in a night-mare; but at last they reached the far perimeter of the field. Together they stepped out into the open air.

In front of them, more vast than they could have imag-ined, were the two glowing domes. There was no evidence that anyone was guarding them. No vehicles, so sounds, no signs warning off trespassers. For a moment the two agents stood staring at the eerie structures. Then they hurried cau-tiously toward the nearer of the two.

A heavy steel door served as entrance—no lock, no alarm system. Mulder pulled it, slowly and with some effort. It opened with a sucking sound, suggesting that the interior was pressurized. He shot Scully a curious look, then stepped inside, Scully at his heels.

Immediately they both jumped, crying out as large fans overhead sent blasts of air down onto them. There was a thunderous roar, and they lunged ahead, into the echoing stillness of the space beyond.

"Cool in here," said Scully, shivering as she tugged at her jacket. She blinked; the dome was so painfully bright it was as though daylight reigned here, though she could see no lamps anywhere. "Temperature's being regulated. . . ."

"For the purpose of *what?*"

Mulder let his head fall back so that he was staring directly overhead. A dizzying web of cross wires and cables was strung there, giving an overall impression of simplicity and some perfect, unknown, function. When he looked down he saw a floor that was the earthbound counterpart to this high-wire act: gray and flat, of metal or some sort of sturdy resinous compound, and utterly featureless. All around them the air was still, but as the two agents moved cautiously through the dome, they gradually became aware of a sound. A steady, resonating hum—almost an electrical hum, but with a slightly different vibration that Mulder couldn't quite put a name to, as though the air channeled some energy that pulsed at a higher or lower frequency than was humanly recognizable.

They headed toward the middle of the vast open space, stepping with care on the gray surface underfoot, until they reached a dividing line where the floor gave way to the dome's epicenter, a space the size of a sports arena.

Before them, laid out in a grid and low to the ground, was row after row of what looked like boxes, sides touching as though they were pieces in some mammoth puzzle or game board. Each was about three feet square, with a dim pewter sheen. Mulder stepped very carefully onto one. It felt reassuringly solid, and after a moment Scully followed him, walking across the grid.

"I think we're on top of something, a large structure," Scully said when they paused to look around. She stared down, frowning. It was apparent now that the boxes had louvered tops, but these were all firmly shut, so that whatever was inside could not be seen. She tapped gently at the box with her foot. "I think these are some kind of venting—"

Mulder stooped, to rest his head against the top of one box, listening. "You hear that?"

"I hear a humming. Like electricity. High voltage, maybe." She gazed overhead, at the bizarre crosshatch of cables and struts and girders spanning the interior of the dome.

"Maybe," said Mulder. "Maybe not."

Scully pointed skyward. "What do you think *those* are for?"

Above them, at the very top of the dome, were two huge louver vents corresponding to the smaller ones underfoot.

"I don't know," said Mulder, scrambling back up again.

They stood side by side, gazing at the ceiling when, without warning, a hollow metallic *bang* echoed through the dome.

In the dome's ceiling one of the vents was opening. As though some great invisible hand was there, the great metal louvers were straining from their flat, closed position, until they pointed straight up and down. Open, so that Scully and Mulder could see a black slab of night beyond, and feel the chill air edging through the gap in the dome. When the first louver was completely open, the second began the same ominous performance, sliding until another series of apertures gaped onto the night. Mulder stared at it, mind racing as he tried to come up with some explanation for what was above them.

Cooling vents? But the dome was already chilly, the temperature maintained by some unseen refrigeration system. Brow furrowed, he looked down and around, searching for something that might provide a clue. His gaze stopped when it came to the mysterious boxes underfoot.

Something occurred to him then. Something extremely unpleasant. Something frightening.

"Scully . . . ?"

His partner continued to stare upward. "Yeah . . . ?"

He grabbed her hand. *"Run."*

He pulled her after him and she followed; not knowing why, heading for the door where they had entered, a good hundred yards away.

She hesitated and looked back at the gray ranks of louvered boxes on the floor, and saw what they were hiding.

One by one the vents on each box opened, domino-style, sliding back until their contents were exposed. And with a sound like a chain saw ripping through new wood, bees emerged: thousands upon thousands of them, pouring from the boxes and streaming toward the open ceiling. Scully drew her hands before her face and turned, staggering after Mulder. He pulled his jacket up around his head and she did the same, clumsily, stumbling as the insects streamed around her. She could see bees clinging to her jacket, her legs; bees swarming so thickly in the air before her that it was like looking through dark gauze.

"Keep going!" Mulder shouted, voice muffled by his sleeve. Scully lurched after him. The entrance was only a few yards away now, but she was falling behind, losing her bearings as the frantically humming swarm descended around her.

Mulder looked as though he were swimming through the cloud of insects, arms flailing, head down. He was nearing the entryway when he turned to see Scully flagging behind him. Bees covered her like a softly rippling pelt. She moved as in slow motion, dazed and terrified.

"Scully!"

She couldn't even lift her head to acknowledge him. Mulder took a deep breath, then raced back to her side. His hand shot out and grabbed her coat, heedless of the bees crawling there. Then he dragged her after him to where the door fans blasted away the insects stubbornly clinging to her body.

He kicked the door open and shoved her out ahead of him. As they went outside, he asked her if she got stung. "I don't think so."

The night came as a shock, after the false daylight of the dome. But before they could catch their breath something else came through the darkness. Not bees this time, but two blinding blades of light bearing down on them. The rushing whir of turbine engines filled the air as two unmarked helicopters came roaring from behind the other dome. They skimmed above the ground, searchlights blazing, headed right for Scully and Mulder.

The agents fled. Bolting out of sight just as the helicopters blasted over the spot where they had stood seconds before. They headed for the cornfields, darting in between the towering rows and knocking away any stalks or leaves that blocked their way. Directly overhead the choppers swooped, searchlights cutting through the cornrows like twin lasers. Mulder and Scully ran in and out of the rows, barely managing to avoid the beams. The helicopters criss-crossed the air above them, like two great insects escaped from that other swarm, banking sharply as they searched the fields below. The wash from their propeller blades ripped through the cornstalks like a tornado, revealing anything that might be hidden within.

In the field Mulder gasped for breath as dust and pollen coated his mouth and nostrils. He staggered down another row, ducking as the searchlight beam swept just overhead but escaping detection—for the moment. He drew up beneath a broken cornstalk and coughed, covering his mouth, then looked around for Scully.

She was gone. Desperation edged out fear as he plunged back into the row, shielding his eyes as he peered between the endless lines of corn.

"*Mulder!*"

She was somewhere ahead of him. Mulder crashed through the field, gasping when he saw one of the choppers hovering into view. "Scully!" he yelled. "Scully!" He kept calling her name as he ran. The chopper hung in the air for a moment as though considering which way to go, then swung around and quickly, relentlessly, beared down upon him.

Before him the ranks of cornstalks thinned. A black ridge appeared, untouched by the helicopter's beams: the edge of the field. His heart pounded as he made a final effort, racing toward open ground. Behind him the chopper roared, cornstalks crashing in its wake. Mulder reached the end of the field and crashed out into the night.

He staggered to a halt, breathing in huge gulps of air. For a moment he could think of nothing else, but then another helicopter thundered up from behind him. He turned, and saw Scully a few feet away.

"Scully?"

"Mulder!" she said, sprinting toward him. "Let's go—"

They broke into a run, racing side by side toward the hillside that hid their car. When they reached the hill, they climbed, frantically, loose stones and dirt streaming down behind them. It was only when they reached the summit that they slowed and looked at each other in the darkness.

Real darkness, starlit and ominously quiet. The helicopters had disappeared.

"Where'd they go?" Scully coughed, wiping her eyes.

"I don't know." Mulder stood for a moment, surveying the plateau below them: the weirdly glowing domes and acres of ravaged corn. Then he turned and continued running, back to the bluff where their car was parked. Scully followed.

The desert's uncanny silence hung over them as they finally reached the car. They rushed to it and jumped inside, Mulder twisting the ignition and pounding on the gas.

It didn't start.

"Shit," he groaned. He turned the key again—nothing.

Waited and did the same—still nothing. Again and again he tried, frantically now, while Scully looked back through the rear window.

"Mulder!"

From behind the bluff rose one of the black helicopters. Suddenly the car's engine roared to life. Mulder threw it into gear and spun out, tires screaming as he turned the car and sent it churning back down the hillside without turning on the lights. Scully stared back breathlessly, waiting for the helicopter to give chase.

It did not. It hovered for a few seconds, then, as silently as it had appeared, it banked and flew off into the night.

CHAPTER

10

FBI HEADQUARTERS
J. EDGAR HOOVER BUILDING
WASHINGTON, D.C.

Assistant Director Jana Cassidy did *not* like to be kept waiting. For the tenth time she rifled through the papers on the table before her, glancing tight-lipped at the closed door to the hearing room. At the table alongside her the other panel members made a point of avoiding her eyes. Cassidy sighed impatiently and looked at her watch, then up again as the door swung open.

Assistant Director Walter Skinner stuck his head in. "She's coming in," he said wearily.

Skinner withdrew to let Scully pass. She had on the same clothes she'd been wearing for two days now, and she brushed surreptitiously at the stubborn bits of cornstalk and pollen that clung burrlike to her jacket. As she entered she dipped her head, smoothing out her hair as she approached the table; then looked up to give the hearing committee a chastened look as she took her seat. Skinner came in behind her and joined the others at the table.

"Special Agent Scully," Cassidy began, reshuffling her papers.

"I apologize for making you wait," Scully broke in. She shot Assistant Director Cassidy a polite look. "But I've brought some new evidence with me—"

"Evidence of what?" Cassidy asked sharply.

Scully reached into the satchel at her feet and pulled out a vinyl evidence bag. She gazed at it reluctantly. When she finally spoke, her tone was anything but confident.

"These are fossilized bone fragments I've been able to study, gathered from the bomb site in Dallas. . . ."

Cassidy scrutinized her coolly, but she didn't take note of the other thing Scully had brought back with her from Texas. Beneath the young agent's mass of auburn hair a bee crawled, as though stretching its legs from the long journey. It hovered momentarily against the navy fabric.

"You've been to Dallas?"

Scully met the other woman's challenging gaze. "Yes."

"Are you going to let us in on *what*, exactly, you're trying to prove?"

"That the bombing in Dallas may have been arranged to destroy the bodies of those firemen, so that their deaths and the reason for them wouldn't have to be explained—"

Unnoticed, the bee disappeared from sight again beneath the collar of Scully's suit jacket.

Cassidy's eyes narrowed: "Those are very serious allegations, Agent Scully."

Scully stared at her hands. "Yes, I know."

There was a hush of murmured responses to this, the panel members turning to confer with each other in low voices. In his chair, Assistant Director Skinner shifted uneasily, watching Scully and trying to figure out just what the hell she'd come up with this time.

Cassidy leaned back and regarded Scully. "And you have conclusive evidence of this? Something to tie this claim of yours to the crime?"

Scully met her gaze, then dropped her eyes. "Nothing completely conclusive," she admitted grudgingly. "But I hope to. We're working to develop this evidence—"

"Working with?"

Scully hesitated. "Agent Mulder."

At Jana Cassidy's knowing nod, the other panel members all shifted again in their chairs. The assistant director looked at Scully, then indicated the door.

"Will you wait outside for a moment, Agent Scully? We need to discuss this matter."

Very slowly Scully stood. She picked up her satchel and walked to the door, glancing back in time to see the look Skinner gave her, a look compounded equally of sympathy and disappointment.

CASEY'S BAR
SOUTHEAST WASHINGTON, D.C.

It was late afternoon when Fox Mulder pushed open the door to Casey's. Inside, it might have been the middle of the night. The same few, bleary-eyed regulars sat and talked. Mulder ignored them all, scanning the back of the room, where a Budweiser sign blinked fitfully above a lone figure slumped in a high-backed wooden booth. When Mulder sat down next to him the man jumped, then quickly leaned over to grab the agent's hand.

"You found something?" Kurtzweil wheezed.

"Yes. On the Texas border. Some kind of experiment. Something they excavated was brought there in tanker trucks."

"What?"

"I'm not sure. A virus—"

"You saw this experiment?" Kurtzweil broke in excitedly.

Mulder nodded. "Yes. But we were chased off."

"What did it look like?"

"There were bees. And corn crops." Kurtzweil stared at him, then laughed with nervous delight. Mulder opened his hands in a helpless gesture. "What *are* they?"

The doctor slid from his seat. "What do you think?"

Mulder looked thoughtful. "A transportation system," he said at last. "Transgenic crops. The pollen genetically altered to carry a virus."

"That would be my guess."

"Your *guess*?" Mulder exploded. "You mean you didn't *know*?"

Kurtzweil didn't reply. Without looking back he headed for the back of the bar. Mulder gaped, then hurried after him, as the few other patrons turned to see what the commotion was.

He caught up with Kurtzweil near the bathrooms. "What do you mean, your *guess*?" he demanded.

Kurtzweil said nothing and continued to head for the back door. With a frustrated sound Mulder collared him, yanking the older man so that the two were inches apart.

"You told me *you had the answers*."

Kurtzweil shrugged. "Yeah, well, I don't have them all."

"You've been *using* me—"

"*I've* been using *you*?" Now it was Kurtzweil's turn to sound offended.

"You didn't know my father—"

The doctor shook his head. "I told you—he and I were old friends."

"You're a liar," Mulder spat. "You lied to me to gather information for you. For your goddamn books. Didn't you?" He shoved the older man against the bathroom door. "Didn't you?"

Suddenly the door swung open. A man hastily exited, making his way between them. As he did so, Kurtzweil broke away and hurried out the back door. Mulder stared after him, then quickly followed.

"Kurtzweil!"

He blinked in the blaze of afternoon light, looking around vain in for his prey. After a moment he sighted him, and Mulder took off. *"Hey!"*

When he came up alongside Kurtzweil, the older man turned on him with unexpected ferocity.

"You'd be shit out of luck if not for me," he gasped, pushing at Mulder's chest. "You saw what you saw because *I led you to it.* I'm putting my ass on the line for you."

"*Your* ass?" Mulder's voice crackled with disdain. "I just got chased across Texas by two black helicopters—"

"And why do you think it is that you're standing here talking to me? These people don't make mistakes, Agent Mulder."

Kurtzweil spun on his heel and strode off. Mulder gazed at him, dumbfounded by the logic of this, when his attention was abruptly shaken by a noise above him. He whirled and looked up to see a figure straddling a fire escape. A tall man, only his legs and feet clearly in sight; but it was obvious he had been watching them. As Mulder moved back to get a better view the man turned and stared down at him, then ducked into an open window and disappeared.

It was only a glimpse, but something about the figure was familiar. His height, the close-cropped hair . . .

Mulder frowned and ran a hand wearily across his forehead, then hurried down the alley after Kurtzweil.

He was gone. Breathlessly Mulder chugged onto the sidewalk, scanning the street and surrounding buildings. Kurtzweil was nowhere to be seen. For several minutes he walked around, searching for any sign of the familiar raincoat and stooped gray head. But finally he had to admit it: Kurtzweil had given him the slip.

When he reached his apartment Mulder jammed the key into the lock and hurried inside, forgetting to close the door behind him. He tossed his jacket on the couch and crossed quickly to his desk, yanking open one drawer after another until at last he discovered what he wanted: a stack of photo albums. One after another he opened them, glancing at the Polaroids and faded 4x5s in their plastic sleeves and then dropping each book on the floor.

Until he found it. An album with peeling daisy decals on the cover, its contents spilling out as he tore it open. Inside, page after page of photos taken during his Wonder Years: lawn sprinklers and summer camp, fishing at the lake and his sister Samantha's fifth birthday party. Fox and

Samantha on the first day of school. Fox and Samantha and their mother. Samantha with their dog.

And there, alongside pictures of his parents and cousins he hadn't seen in decades, a family barbecue. His mother kneeling on the lawn between Fox and his sister; above them their father at the grill, smiling. At his side a tall man with dark hair, lean-faced, smiling as well, not stooped at all and younger, oh much younger.

Alvin Kurtzweil.

A knock shattered his reverie. Mulder turned, dazed, and looked up to see Scully standing in the open door of his apartment. Her eyes met his.

"What?" He got to his feet, scattering photos around him. "Scully? What's wrong?"

"Salt Lake City, Utah," she said softly. "Transfer effective immediately."

He shook his head, refusing to hear her.

"I already gave Skinner my letter of resignation," she added brokenly.

Mulder stared at her. "You can't quit, Scully."

"I can, Mulder. I debated whether or not to even tell you in person, because I knew—"

He took a step toward her and then stopped, gesturing at the photos at his feet. "We're close to something here," he said, his voice rising desperately. "We're on the verge—"

"*You're* on the verge, Mulder." She blinked and looked away. "Please—please don't do this to me."

He continued to gaze at her. Not believing she was here, not believing this could be it. "After what you saw last night," he said at last, "after all you've seen, Scully— You can't just walk away."

"I have. I did. It's done."

He shook his head, stunned. "Just like that . . ."

"I'm contacting the state board Monday to file my medical reinstatement papers—"

"But I *need* you on this, Scully!" he said urgently.

"You don't, Mulder. You've never needed me. I've only held you back." She forced herself to look away from him, biting her lip to keep herself from crying. She turned and started for the door. "I've got to go."

He caught her before she reached the elevator, running to keep up with her. "You're wrong," he cried.

Scully turned on him. "*Why* was I assigned to you?" she asked fiercely. "To *debunk your work*. To rein you in. To shut you down."

He shook his head. "No. You've saved me, Scully." He put his hands lightly on her shoulders and gazed down into her open blue eyes. "As difficult and frustrating as it's been sometimes, your goddamn strict rationalism and science have saved me—a hundred times, a *thousand* times. You've—you've kept me honest and made me whole. I owe you so much, Scully, and you owe me nothing."

He dipped his head, a knot in his throat as he went on in a voice barely above a whisper. "I don't want to do this without you. I don't know if I can. And if I quit now, they win. . . ."

He gazed down at her and she stared back at him, silent, her blue eyes dark in the half light. She moved very slightly away from him, not breaking his gaze; her own registering respect and sorrow. His hands remained barely touching her arms as she lifted herself on tiptoe and kissed his forehead.

He did not move away, did not for a moment respond. Their eyes met and linked. A sudden, inexplicable tension flared. And then his hands tightened on her, his head dipped as he drew her toward him, his fingers moving upward to trace the long line of her neck, her skin warm beneath the thick mane of auburn hair, her cheek. For only an instant she hesitated, then reached for him. She could feel his mouth grazing hers, when—

"Ouch!" Scully pulled away from Mulder, rubbing her neck where his hand had been.

"I'm sorry." Mulder stared at her, worried he had done something wrong.

Scully's voice was thick. "I think . . . something . . . stung me."

She withdrew her hand as Mulder moved around her, running his fingers quickly across her neck. He shook his head. "It must've gotten in your shirt."

He gasped as Scully slumped forward, as he hastily caught her in his arms. Her head lolled drunkenly as Mulder whispered, frightened, "Scully . . ."

She stared up at him through slit eyes and opened her

hand. In the palm lay a bumblebee, legs feebly twitching. "Something's wrong," she murmured, barely coherent. "I'm having . . . lancinating pain . . . my chest. My . . . motor functions are being affected. I'm—"

Frantically, but as gently as he could, Mulder lowered her until she lay upon the floor. She felt limp and helpless as a sleeping child, her head rolling to one side. She continued to speak, her voice growing fainter and fainter, eyes no longer focusing.

". . . my pulse feels thready and I—I've got a funny taste in the back of my throat."

Mulder knelt above her, straining to hear. "I think you're in anaphylactic shock—"

"No—it's—"

"Scully . . ." Mulder's voice cracked.

"I've got no allergy," she whispered. "Something . . . this . . . Mulder . . . I think . . . I think you should call an ambulance. . . ."

He stumbled to his feet and raced for the phone, punching in 911. "This is Special Agent Fox Mulder. I have an emergency. I have an agent down—"

Scant minutes passed before he heard sirens wailing outside. He ignored the elevator and ran downstairs, holding the door open as two paramedics rushed past him carrying a folded gurney. He followed them, giving them a broken version of all that had occurred. When they reached Scully, one paramedic opened the gurney while the other knelt beside her.

"Can you hear me?" he said in a loud voice. "Can you say your name?"

Scully's lips moved but no words came out. The paramedic shot a look at his partner. "She's got constriction in the throat and larynx." He looked back down at her and asked, "Are you breathing okay?"

No reply. He lay his head beside her mouth, listening. "Passages are open. Let's get her in the van."

They bundled her onto the gurney and Mulder went with them back into the corridor. Neighbors were standing in doorways, staring as the paramedics hustled the gurney toward the elevator.

"Coming through, people! Here we go, coming through—"

Mulder rode with them down the elevator and ran outside to where the EMT van waited, lights flashing. The paramedics banged out the front door, stutter-stepping the gurney down the front walk. Mulder ran after them.

"She said she had a taste in the back of her throat," he said. "But there was no preexisting allergy to bee stings. The bee that stung her may have been carrying a virus—"

The second paramedic stared at him. "A virus?"

"Get on the radio," the first medic shouted at the van driver. "Tell them we have a cytogenic reaction, we need an advise and administer—"

They guided the gurney to the back of the vehicle, lifting it in with expert hands. Scully's eyes rolled and then focused on Mulder. Unable to communicate, she held his gaze as they rolled her into the brightly lit interior. The paramedic quickly moved into the van. Before Mulder could climb aboard and join Scully, the paramedics swung the doors closed.

"Hey—what hospital are you taking her to?" he said as the doors were closing.

He ran to the driver's side of the van, waving frantically. Mulder knocked on the window.

"What hospital are you taking her to?"

He got his first look at the driver, a tall man in a light blue EMT uniform, his hair close-cropped. He stared coldly out at Mulder, who drew up short in shock.

Because suddenly, in a split second, it all fell together. It was the uniform that triggered his memory: the tall man on the fire escape, sliding into an open window; the tall man in a vendor's uniform exiting the snack room where the bomb had been. And now the driver of the van . . .

It was the same man. His hand was raised, aiming a handgun directly at Mulder. The next instant a blast echoed through the night. Mulder fell backward, clutching his head as the ambulance shrieked away. He lay bleeding in the street and his neighbors watched, horrified, as a second ambulance roared up, skidding to a halt to let two other paramedics leap out and rush to the fallen man's side.

•   •   •

NATIONAL AIRPORT
WASHINGTON, D.C.

An hour later an unmarked auxiliary truck sat on the runway overlooking Haines Point, its engine idling. In the distance a private Gulfstream jet emerged from an unmarked hangar and taxied slowly down the tarmac. At sight of the Gulfstream, the truck's engines cut off. Two men in black fatigues hopped down from the cab and swiftly moved to the rear of the vehicle. They opened the doors and carefully, deftly, removed a large translucent container, a cryobubble, its exterior a crazy grid of monitors and gauges, oxygen tanks and refrigeration units. A thin layer of frost coated its interior, and behind this, dimly seen as though through fog, lay Scully. Her body strapped in, her limbs and torso so still she might have been dead; save that as the men carried the container from the truck, her eyes moved every so slightly, blinking.

The Gulfstream turned and rolled toward the truck, nosing through the darkness. When it was perhaps twenty feet from the waiting truck it halted. The men moved even more quickly then, bearing the container and its human cargo to the jet. As they did a door on the plane opened. Steps unfolded down to the runway, and a moment later man appeared. He stood at the top of the stairs, watching, then withdrew a pack of cigarettes from his jacket and lit one. He stood there for a minute, smoking, as the men brought the container to the cargo hold and loaded it inside.

When they were finished the men turned and hurried back to the truck. The Cigarette-Smoking Man dropped his cigarette onto the tarmac and reboarded the aircraft. The steps retracted, the plane swung around and headed for the central runway. Ten minutes later its lights could be seen arcing through the night as it arrowed above the city.

CHAPTER

11

INTENSIVE CARE UNIT
GEORGE WASHINGTON UNIVERSITY MEDICAL CENTER
WASHINGTON, D.C.

"I think he's coming out . . ."

"He is—he's coming to!"

"Hey, Mulder . . ."

In his bed, Mulder blinked painfully. It hurt even to

think about opening his eyes, so for a long time he didn't; he only lay there listening to the voices above him. Men's voices, vaguely familiar.

"Mulder . . . ?"

He opened his eyes. Above him, ringed by hospital lights and banks of monitoring equipment, three faces were framed by the ceiling. "Oh god . . ." Mulder moaned.

Langly shook his head, his long hair falling in his face. "What's wrong?" Beside him the diminutive Frohike and Byers, courtly as ever, gazed at the agent in concern.

"Tin Man," Mulder whispered in amazement, staring first at Byers, then Langly. "Scarecrow—"

He raised his head slightly, indicating Frohike. "—Toto." He winced, then sat up, gingerly rubbing his face and frowning at the bandage there. "What am I doing here?"

"You were shot in the head," Byers explained in a low voice. "The bullet broke the flesh on your right brow and glanced off your temporal plate."

Mulder ran a finger over the bandage. "Penetration but not perforation," he said woozily.

Langly nodded. "Three centimeters to the left and we'd all be playing harps."

"They gave you a craniotomy to relieve the pressure from a subdural hematoma," Byers went on. "But you've been unconscious since they brought you in."

"Your guy Skinner's been with you around the clock," said Frohike.

Langly broke in, "We got the news and made a trip to your apartment. Found a bug in your phone line—"

To illustrate, Byers dangled a minuscule microphone in front of Mulder's face.

"*And* one in your hall," Frohike added. He held up a small vial containing a bumblebee.

Mulder stared at it, eyes widening as his memory flooded back. "Scully had a violent reaction to a bee sting—"

"Right," said Byers. "And you called 911. Except that call was intercepted."

Mulder shook his head. "They took her—"

He pushed the covers off, moving shakily as he tried to swing his legs to the ground. As he did so, the door to his room opened a bit. Assistant Director Walter Skinner peeked in, his expression changing from concern to surprise when he saw Mulder standing up.

"Agent Mulder!"

Mulder looked up, nearly losing his balance in the process. "Where's Scully?" he asked thickly. Langly grabbed his shoulder to keep him from falling.

Skinner came into the room, carefully shutting the door behind him. He crossed to Mulder's side and regarded him for a long moment before saying flatly, "She's missing. We've been unable to locate her or the vehicle they took her in."

"Whoever they are—" Mulder's voice shook, and Langly tightened his hold on him protectively. "—this goes right back to Dallas. It goes right back to the bombing."

Skinner nodded. "I know." At Mulder's stunned look he went on, "Agent Scully reported your suspicions to OPR. On the basis of her report, I sent techs over to SAC Michaud's apartment. They picked up PETN residues on his personal affects—and analysis showed the residue was consistent with the construction of the vending machine device in Dallas."

Mulder sat back down on the bed, his head reeling. "How deep does this go?"

"I don't know."

For a minute Mulder just sat there, taking it all in. When he lifted his head again, he saw a figure momentarily framed in the small window of the room door. A man in a suit, casting a furtive glance in to where Mulder, Skinner, and the Lone Gunmen were gathered. The stranger stared at them, then hurried off. Mulder quickly turned back to Skinner.

"Are we being watched?"

"I'm not taking any chances."

Mulder nodded. He pulled tentatively at the bandage on his head, grimaced and then peeled it away, revealing the still-livid wound. He tossed the bandage away and looked at one of the Lone Gunmen. "I need your clothes, Byers."

Byers started. "Me?"

Skinner frowned. "What are you doing, Agent Mulder?"

Already Mulder was undoing his hospital gown, angling himself behind Frohike as he ducked toward the bathroom. "I've got to find Scully."

"Do you know where she is?" asked Frohike.

"No." Mulder dropped his hospital gown and motioned anxiously at Byers. "But I know someone who might have an answer. . . ."

"Who better," he ended with grim determination, as reluctantly Byers began to remove his clothes.

A short while later the door to Mulder's room opened. First Langly and then Frohike stepped out into the corridor, glancing around nervously as behind them a third figure appeared, clad in Byers's jacket and natty tie. Standing a few feet away, his back to them, a man in a suit leaned against the wall reading a newspaper. As they started down the hall the man in the suit looked up. He glanced at them, then casually turned and drifted toward Mulder's room, his eyes revealing his suspicions as he peered through the little glass window.

Inside, tucked into the hospital bed with the sheets pulled up to his nose, a figure lay motionless. Beside him Walter Skinner stood talking on the phone. The man in the suit stared at the bed, frowning, then turned to look back down the hall again.

At the end of the corridor the three men walked quickly, Langly and Frohike flanking Mulder. As they rounded the corner Frohike covertly passed him a cell phone. Without hesitation, Mulder punched in Dr. Kurtzweil's number.

CHAPTER 12

CASEY'S BAR
SOUTHEAST WASHINGTON, D.C.

In the dark alley behind Casey's, Alvin Kurtzweil waited anxiously, scanning the night for any sign of Fox Mulder. When he saw no sign of him, he turned and started back for the door, reaching for the knob. He twisted it and

137

stepped inside, and came up short against a sparely elegant man in a cashmere overcoat, his hands raised in mock surprise and delight to find Kurtzweil there.

"Dr. Kurtzweil, isn't it? Dr *Alvin* Kurtzweil?"

"Jesus Christ . . ." Kurtzweil gasped and reached behind him for the door. He glanced around fearfully, trying to edge back outside, but the Well-Manicured Man only smiled.

"You're surprised. But certainly you've been expecting some response to your indiscretion . . ."

Kurtzweil shook his head furiously. "I didn't tell him anything."

"I'm quite sure that whatever you told Agent Mulder, you have your good reasons," the other man said evenly. "It's a weakness in men our age: the urge to confess." He paused, then added, "I have much to confess myself."

Kurtzweil stared at him, confused by his words and serene tone. Finally he blurted, "What are you doing here? What do you want from me?"

"I'd hoped to try and help you understand. What I'm here to do, is to try and protect my children. That's all. You and I have but short lives left. I can only hope that the same isn't true for them."

He stood quite calmly and held the door open, as if in invitation. Kurtzweil stood there for a moment, as though considering the other man's words; then suddenly bolted, pushing past him and back into the alley. He ran toward the street, but had gone only a few paces when headlights blinded him. A town car pulled into the alley, accelerating as it roared down the narrow corridor. Kurtzweil stopped, panting, and squinted at the approaching car. He turned to stare with terrified eyes at the man still standing calmly in the doorway.

Fox Mulder barreled through the front door of Casey's, looking around frenziedly for Kurtzweil. The bar was crowded, more people than he'd ever seen there. He elbowed past them, pausing to get his bearings and peer vainly through the dim room. There was no sign of Kurtzweil anywhere. Mulder sighed, ran his hand through his hair, and hurriedly made his way to the back to the doctor's usual booth.

It was empty. Mulder sucked his breath in, fighting real panic. He turned and ran to the dank hallway where the bathrooms were, edging by a knot of laughing women, and burst out into the alley.

"Shit," he whispered.

A town car sat idling on the cobblestone pavement. At its rear, a tall, beautifully dressed man and his uniformed driver were arranging something in the car's trunk. As Mulder stared, they closed the trunk. The elegant man looked up, and said in greeting, "Mr. Mulder."

Mulder's hands clenched. "What happened to Kurtzweil?"

The Well-Manicured Man shrugged off-handedly. "He's come and gone."

He started toward Mulder and Mulder backed away, still breathing hard. "Where's Scully?"

The Well-Manicured Man stopped a few feet in front of him. He took in Mulder's shoes, the too-short trousers and ill-fitting jacket borrowed from Byers. After a moment he looked up and said, "I have answers for you."

"Is she alive?"

"Yes." The Well-Manicured Man hesitated, then said, "I'm quite prepared to tell you everything, though there isn't much you haven't already guessed."

Mulder's throat felt tight. "About the conspiracy?"

"I think of it as an agreement," the other man said lightly. "A word your father liked to use."

Mulder took a step toward him. "I want to know where Scully is."

The Well-Manicured Man nodded. Mulder tensed as he reached into his jacket pocket, and removed a thin envelope of dark-green felt. The Well-Manicured Man weighed it in his palm, then said, "The location of Agent Scully. And the means to save her life. Please—"

He gestured toward the car, where the driver stood holding the back door open. Mulder hesitated, then stepped toward it. He moved past the Well-Manicured Man and slid into the seat. The older man got in after him and closed the door. He motioned at the driver, and the town car pulled away.

Mulder sat bolt upright, looking guardedly from the man beside him to the driver, who returned his gaze in the rearview mirror. Without a word, the Well-Manicured Man handed Mulder the small felt envelope.

"What is it?" Mulder asked.

"A weak vaccine against the virus Agent Scully has been infected with. It must be administered within ninety-six hours."

Mulder stared at him, then at the felt envelope in his hand. "You're lying."

"No." The Well-Manicured Man stared broodingly out the tinted window. "Though I have no way to prove otherwise. The virus is extraterrestrial. We know very little about it, except that it is the original inhabitant of this planet."

Mulder looked dubious. "A *virus?*"

"A simple, unstoppable life form. What *is* a virus, but a colonizing force that cannot be defeated? Living in a cave underground, until it mutates. And attacks."

"*This* is what you've been trying to conceal?" Mulder no longer tried to keep the contempt from his voice. "A disease?"

"No!" exploded the Well-Manicured Man. "For god's sake, you've got it all *backward*—

"AIDS, the Ebola virus—on an evolutionary scale, they are newborns. *This* virus walked the planet long before the dinosaurs."

Mulder scowled. "What do you mean, 'walked'?"

"Your aliens, Agent Mulder. Your little green men—they arrived here millions of years ago. Those that didn't leave have been lying dormant underground since the last Ice Age, in the form of an evolved pathogen. Just waiting to be reconstituted when the alien race returns to colonize the planet. And using *us* as hosts. Against this we have no defense. Nothing but a weak vaccine . . ."

He paused and stared pointedly at Mulder, who finally looked shaken. "Do you see why it was kept secret, Agent Mulder? Why even the best men—men like your father—could not let the truth be known? Until Dallas, we believed the virus would simply control us. That mass infection would make us a slave race."

"That's why you bombed the building," said Mulder slowly. "The infected firemen . . . the boy . . ."

The Well-Manicured Man nodded grimly. "Imagine our surprise when they began to gestate. My group has been working cooperatively with the alien colonists, facilitating programs like the one you saw. To gain access to the virus, in hope that we might secretly develop a cure."

"To save yourselves," broke in Mulder.

The Well-Manicured Man shrugged. "When war is futile, victory consists of merely staying alive. Survival is the ultimate ideology." He hesitated, then gave Mulder a cool smile. "Your father wisely refused to believe this."

"My father sacrificed my sister!" cried Mulder angrily. "He let them take Samantha—"

"No." For a moment the Well-Manicured Man looked

almost sorrowful. "Without a vaccination, the only true survivors of the viral holocaust would be those immune to it: human/alien clones. He *allowed* your sister to be abducted, to be taken to a cloning program. For one reason."

"So she'd survive," Mulder breathed in sudden understanding. "As a genetic hybrid . . ."

The Well-Manicured Man nodded. "Your father chose hope over selfishness. Hope in the only future he had: his children. His hope for you, Agent Mulder, was that you would uncover the truth about the Project. That you would do everything you could to stop it—

"That you would fight the future."

He fell silent. On the other side of the backseat, Mulder sat stunned, feeling as though all at once his destiny had been validated, or maybe simply justified. "Why are you telling me this?" he said at last.

The Well-Manicured Man stared at his hands for a long time before replying. "For the sake of my own children. Nothing more, nothing less. Once they learn what I've told you, my life will be over."

He raised his head, and Mulder looked up to see the driver staring back at them from the rearview mirror. At their notice he quickly brought his attention back to the road, and Mulder asked, "What happened to Dr. Kurtzweil?"

"His knowledge became too great for his indiscretion. As your father knew, some things need to be sacrificed to the future."

Mulder stared at the other man's impassive face and suddenly realized the truth of it.

"You—you *murdered* him," Mulder said in shocked disbelief. When the Well-Manicured Man said nothing, Mulder grabbed his door handle. "Let me out. Stop the car."

The Well-Manicured Man gestured at the front seat. "Driver . . ."

Slowly the limo pulled to a stop. Outside the street was empty, lit only by a single yellow crime light. There were no houses, no people, only an abandoned gas station flanked by several rusting Dumpsters. Mulder jimmied the handle. It was locked. He whirled to challenge his captor, and found himself looking down at a handgun resting carefully, almost casually, on the other man's leg. Its barrel was aimed directly at Mulder's chest.

"The men I work with will stop at nothing to clear the way for what they believe is their stake in the inevitable future," the Well-Manicured Man said as Mulder recoiled. "I was ordered to kill Dr. Kurtzweil."

Mulder backed against the door as in one fluid motion the other man lifted the gun. "—as I was ordered to kill you." But before Mulder could cry out, the Well-Manicured Man whirled and shot the driver in the head.

Blood spattered the front windshield and Agent Mulder's jacket. He gasped, still trying to comprehend what had just happened, and stared horrified at the man holding the gun beside him. "Trust no one, Mr. Mulder," said the Well-Manicured Man matter-of-factly. Mulder looked at him, expecting to be next. But the Well-Manicured Man only opened the door and stepped from the town car. He stood in the desolate street and held the door open for Mulder, who was still frozen in his seat.

"Get out of the car, Agent Mulder."

"Why? The upholstery is already ruined."

"Get out."

Taking a deep breath, Mulder joined him on the asphalt. He looked down at the felt envelope in his hand. The Well-Manicured Man stared at him with an intensely somber look, still grasping the handgun.

"You have precious little time, Agent Mulder. What I've given you—the alien colonists don't know it exists . . . yet. You have in your hand the power to end the Project. To take what is most valuable from them."

"I need to know *how*—" Mulder cried.

"The vaccine you hold is the only defense against the virus. Its introduction into the alien environment may have the power to destroy the delicate plans we've so assiduously protected for the last fifty years."

"May?" Mulder clutched the envelope and shook his head. "What do you mean *may*?"

"Find Agent Scully. Only then will you realize the scope and grandeur of the Project. And why *you* must save her. Because only her science can save you."

Mulder stared at him, waiting for more. But the Well-Manicured Man only pointed down the street. "Go."

Mulder started to protest, but the other man raised the gun and pointed it at him.

"Go *now!*"

Mulder did. Walking quickly away from the car, then hastening into a run, looking back over his shoulder as he fled. Behind him the Well-Manicured Man stood watching him for a moment; then turned and got back into the car. He shut the door, and Mulder had the faintest glimpse of movement behind the tinted glass. Seconds later, the car exploded.

Mulder's voice was drowned by the roar of flames shooting up from the vehicle. The impact wave knocked him to the ground. He lost his grip on the precious envelope and it briefly flew from his hand into the darkness. Gasping, he struggled to his feet, and reached out for the little dark-green rectangle, its contents spilling onto the street. The light from the blazing car touched what was there: a syringe; small glass ampule, miraculously undamaged; and a tiny piece of paper with numbers meticulously written on it.

BASE 1
SOUTH 83°00 LAT.
EAST 63°00 LONG.
326 FEET

Mulder picked up the envelope and its contents.

CHAPTER

13

POLE OF INACESSIBILITY
ANTARCTICA
48 HOURS LATER

T he ice was so vast and colorless that it blended into the sky, so that there was only white: endless, eternal, terrible. White and devastating cold. Inside the cab of the snow tractor, Mulder's breath turned to vapor thick and white as smoke. Ice crystals formed where several days' worth of beard had sprung out upon his face, coating the edges of his mouth and eyes. Even with the heat blasting inside the cabin, he could barely feel his hands inside their heavy gloves, resting awkwardly on the wheel. He hunched over the controls, focusing all of his energy on what lay before him. The tractor crawled on across the harsh frozen land like an insect, leaving parallel lines behind it to mark its tortured journey across the edge of the Ross Ice Shelf.

Hours passed. In that land without night he lost all track of time, and with no landmarks—no buildings, no mountains, nothing but snow and ice—he grew fearful of losing his bearings as well. Finally he maneuvered the tractor to a stop, reached for the handheld Global Positioning Satellite monitor to check his position. He squinted as numbers scrolled across the GPS monitor's screen. They told him that he had reached his coordinates. Glancing at the dashboard, he saw that the gas gauge hovered just above 'E.' Looking out the front window, there was nothing but snow to see, nothing but white all the way to the horizon. He checked the GPS device one more time, then reached for the door latch and stepped outside.

Snow crunched underfoot, snow whirled around his head. In this forbidding environment, even with the GPS device in his hand, he might as well be taking a space walk—without the security of a lifeline.

He trudged across the ice. The snow squall abated, and

his footprints showed clearly behind him. When he looked back at the snow tractor it looked very small and insubstantial against the endless vista of white ground and steely sky. He began a long, laboring ascent of a gentle grade, now and then sliding and catching himself by digging hands or heels into the soft new snow. When he reached the top of the incline he dropped to his knees, instinctively ducking his head.

Below, spread out across the plain like some misplaced vision of a space colony, was an ice station surrounded by tractors and Sno-Cats and snowmobiles. Mulder pulled a pair of compact high-powered binoculars from his parka and scanned the domes and support vehicles, looking for signs of life. None, until he let his sight linger on the most distant dome.

"Bingo," he whispered.

There, jolting over the ice fields, was another snow tractor. It crept across the barren landscape toward the ice station, coming to a halt beside one of the domed buildings. For several minutes the vehicle sat there, and then a door opened on the dome and a man emerged wearing a parka and fur hat. The man stood on the doorstep for a moment, his face obscured by a cloud of gray vapor. Then he tossed something into the snow and walked to the vehicle.

The Cigarette-Smoking Man. Mulder watched as he yanked on the door of the snow tractor and clambered inside. The vehicle reversed, driving over its tracks in the snow, then slowly crawled off toward the far horizon.

Mulder drew the binoculars back from his eyes. He was breathing even harder now, more excitement than exertion, and had to force himself to sit for several minutes, to calm himself for what was ahead. Finally he pocketed the field glasses, stumbled to his feet, and started down the far side of the slope toward the ice station.

He moved cautiously and with effort, carefully weighing each step before setting foot on the ice crust before him. When he reached the bottom of the slope he glanced furtively behind him, still unable to shake the fear of being followed; then turned and went on.

Mulder's gaze remained fixed on the domes. Ahead of him, the ice station very gradually grew larger as he approached, until the domes loomed up against the cloud-streaked sky. He had only a few hundred yards left to go, when with a cry he stumbled. Beneath one boot the ice crust gave way. There was an instant when the world seemed to trembled before him, the domes like huge bubbles floating atop a milky sea. Then the ice collapsed under him.

He fell, landing on his back. The surface beneath him was cold and hard and smooth. He lay there for a moment, grunting as he caught his breath and trying to determine if he'd broken anything. Pain shot through one arm, and the gun wound at his temple throbbed, but after a minute had passed he rolled over, wincing, and began figuring out where the hell he was.

He had fallen on some hard, narrow, metallic structure, like a catwalk or steel floor. Its dull black hue was in stark contrast to the dead-white of the ice that encased it. There were vents in the floor through which air blew. Warm air only by the relative standards of the Antarctic; but when Mulder lifted his head to gaze upward he saw what had happened. The air had caused a bubble, an air pocket, to form beneath the ice: above him the ceiling had been carved into patterns corresponding to the vents below. Where he had fallen through, the ice had softened and melted enough that it at last gave way at his tread. He rose to his knees, the air from one of the vents blowing onto his face. The vent was open, with no protective grate or covering, and big enough for a man to crawl into. Mulder pulled off the hood of his parka and his gloves, and looked deep into the vent, then back up at the hole he'd fallen through. No way back up there, and nothing around him but solid ice. He gazed back at the vent.

It was his only choice. He took a deep breath, then pulled himself forward into the darkness.

Inside the vent was cold and pitch-black, its sides corrugated to give him easy purchase. He moved cautiously, feeling ahead of him as the ribbed corridor snaked downward, until a pinprick of light appeared. Several more minutes of creeping and he had reached the end, another vent opening into god knows what. He squeezed through headfirst, grabbing at a small ledge that projected beneath him and with difficulty maneuvered his legs until he could swing himself down and then onto the ground.

Mulder blinked and shoved his gloved hand into his pocket, fumbling until he withdrew a flashlight. It clicked on; he swept it up and down in front of him, revealing a terrifying landscape.

He stood in the middle of an endless corridor carved into the ice. To the left and right, as far as he could see, were tall glassy shapes, regularly spaced on both sides of the passageway, like ice coffins stood upright against the cavern walls. He trained the light on the corridor, marking where it curved off into the distance; turned and did the same in the other direction. Then he spun around and pointed it directly in front of him. Mulder reached to brush frost from the surface ice. He gasped at what he saw.

There was a man frozen in the ice. Naked, his eyes open and staring into some long-forgotten distance. His hair was long and dark and matted, his flattened features oddly inhuman: broad nose with flared nostrils, pronounced brow ridge, lips drawn back to show yellowing peglike teeth. Drawing closer he could see that the man's flesh had the same weird translucence as that of the fireman in the morgue. Mulder grimaced, then drew back in revulsion as he saw something *inside* the man: an embryonic creature with huge, oblique black eyes, frozen like its host.

Mulder turned and quickly paced down the dim ice corridor. Where it ended, dim light seeped through several low, arched openings. Mulder dropped to his knees to peer through, and saw before him a brief passage that widened into a sort of balcony. He bellied down on his stomach and pulled himself through the arch, grunting as he scraped against ice and metal. When he reached the other end, he poked his head out onto the balcony and gazed up in wonder.

All around him was space, sweeping to a domed ceiling almost inconceivably high above him. He looked down and fought a wave of vertigo; wherever the bottom was, it was at least as far away as the top. Very carefully he pulled himself out, until he crouched on the lip of the balcony—actually a ventilation port opening onto the empty center of the dome. All around him, circling the dome, were countless other ports; hundreds of them, thousands. Shakily he got to his feet, steadying himself against the wall behind him, and gazed down to the floor of the dome. There, a large central theater glowed with an eerie intensity different from the pale light that emanated elsewhere in the vast space: an icy, almost livid, glow. Leading down to this central theater were several enormous tubular spokes. One of them angled up past Mulder, perhaps an arm's length away.

It took several minutes for all this to sink in. The scale was too immense, much huger than anything Mulder had ever seen, could even imagine seeing. But strangest and most terrifying of all was what he saw within that central space: row upon row of roughly man-sized pods, dark-colored, hanging in formation from long railings that extended into the darkness. He squinted, trying to figure out what they were, and where the seemingly endless rows led; while hundreds of feet above Mulder, another figure gazed in disbelief at what was before him. Within the heated cab of his Sno-Cat, the Cigarette-Smoking Man leaned forward to clear a spot on the foggy windshield. Behind him the outlines of the ice station could barely be seen; before him a vague shape grew more distinct, until at last he could see it clearly—

The snow tractor Mulder had abandoned on the ice.

For a long moment, the Cigarette-Smoking Man gazed at the tractor. Then, without a word, he turned his own vehicle, and as quickly as he could, he drove back to the base.

Beneath the ice, Mulder continued to peer into the dimness, tracing the rows of frozen objects in an attempt to determine their origin. As he did so, he noticed that in the furthest recesses of the dome, the rows appeared to be moving. The objects suspended from the railings slid along slowly and rhythmically, one by one clicking into place as though part of some gargantuan machine. He blinked, trying to get a better view, and then saw what he had not noticed before.

On the floor hundreds of feet below him, and within the shadow of those moving rows, lay a discarded cryolitter. Its plastic top had been removed and lay discarded alongside it. Amidst the dull gray bulwarks and stark, commanding architecture of the dome, it looked surprisingly small and frail, the sole artifact made to human scale. And because of that, it unsettled Mulder more than almost anything else he had seen.

His face grim, he tore his gaze away and once more stared at the long tubelike structure that rose a few feet behind him. It had a small opening, just wide enough that a man might fit inside. Without stopping to think of the danger, Mulder slipped inside.

It was tight, but he could fit. He began to climb down, struggling to see in the near-darkness, hands and feet slipping as he tried to gain purchase. The tube felt slippery, almost oily, to the touch, but there were small protuberances like rivets which he could steady himself on. He climbed down for what seemed like hours, fighting exhaustion, when without warning his hands slipped and he began to slide. He struggled futilely to stop, but continued until he reached the end of the tube and found himself striking a narrow ledge. He scrambled desperately at last managing to hold on.

His breath shuddering, he looked downward. As he did so the binoculars slipped from his pocket and fell. He watched them fall, light glinting as they twisted and turned. He waited for the sound of their impact, waited and waited and then held his breath, to make sure he wouldn't miss the sound of them hitting bottom.

He heard nothing. There was no bottom; or if there was, it was so far below him as to be the yawning chasm of a true abyss. He looked downward and saw an unimaginably black and bottomless pit. The sight terrified him. With every ounce of strength that remained, Mulder pulled himself along the ledge, his fingers digging into the slick material, until finally he managed to lift himself up, and then over, onto the inner side.

He took a deep breath, then got to his feet. He was in a sort of corridor, darker and warmer than the one he had left, its walls glistening faintly. He pulled out his flashlight and trained its beam on the tunnel. He walked carefully following the faint beam of light until he saw before him the cryolitter. He approached it hesitantly, and when he reached it he stood for a long moment. Inside were Scully's clothes and the little gold cross she always wore around her neck. He stooped and picked up the cross, pocketed it, and went on.

It was as though he were inside some hellish abattoir. Throughout the entire length of the corridor, a metal rack was suspended from the ceiling. Hanging from the rack were the pods—the objects he had seen on the upper level. But here it was warm enough that they were not completely frozen. He walked along slowly, his flashlight tracing the outlines of what each cryopod held: a human body, barely visible behind a very thin sheath of green ice.

But the faces that stared out from these pods were not the crude, proto-human visages of the thing he had seen above. These were men and women like himself. Each had a disturbingly organic-looking tube protruding from his or her mouth. Their eyes were wide, gazing out with blind, confused horror, as though they still looked upon whatever dreadful apparatus had frozen them alive.

Rapt with dread, Mulder walked alongside this malign

carousel, staring at first one face, then another. Trying not to admit to himself, even now, what he was looking for—who he was looking for—until he saw her.

"Oh, Christ," he whispered.

He drew up short in front of a wall of green ice. There, within one of the frozen cysts, her features unmistakable, was Scully. Her russet hair rimmed with snow, her eyes turned heavenward. A tube protruded from her mouth, and she had a look of horror on her face.

Fighting his own horror, Mulder struck the cryopod with his flashlight, smashing it against the icy covering again and again: nothing. Remembering the cryolitter in the distance he ran to it, grabbed one of the oxygen tanks from its lid, and raced back to Scully. Grunting with effort, he raised the tank and drove it repeatedly against the cryopod.

With a muffled *crack* the pod shattered. Ice and slush pooled onto the ground, and for the first time he saw Scully clearly, her body shrouded with frost. With shaking fingers he unzipped his jacket and felt for the envelope in the inner pocket. He pulled out the syringe and ampoule, wrestling with the rubber cap and squinting to see the needle in the darkness. Then he jabbed it into her shoulder.

Almost instantly, viscous amber fluid oozed from the tube in her mouth, thick as melted tar. Then the tube began to shrivel, the desiccation moving from where it entered her mouth all the way to the cryopod that had enclosed her. At the same moment the tunnel shuddered.

Mulder lurched and nearly crashed into the wall. He steadied himself, then yanked the tube from Scully's mouth.

Her eyes blinked, her lips moved as she tried to suck in air. Rapture gave way to fear as her eyes rolled, trying to focus, and still the air would not reach her lungs.

"Breathe!" Mulder cried. "Can you breathe?"

Before him she strained, her expression desperate, like a swimmer struggling to come up for air. Then amber liquid suddenly poured from her mouth. She began to cough and gag, taking huge gulps of air as her eyes finally focused on Mulder, as though he were a phantom—or a miracle. Her mouth worked as she tried to speak, whispered words that Mulder couldn't discern.

"What?" He leaned into her tenderly, putting his ear against her cold mouth. The softest sound imaginable came out.

"Cold—"

"Hang on," said Mulder grimly. "I'm going to get you out of here."

Gently he pulled her from the cryopod and laid her on the floor, then began peeling away the outer layers of his own clothing—his socks, his hooded parka, his protective outer pants—and put them onto her.

•   •   •

Inside the ice station the room began to shake. The Cigarette-Smoking Man hurried past row upon row of computers where men sat, their eyes fixed on the blinking screens. In front of one monitor, a man looked up worriedly as the Cigarette-Smoking Man hastened to his side.

The man pointed at the screen, where a complex system of graphs had suddenly changed, numbers and levels skyrocketing. "We've got a contaminant in the system," he said.

The Cigarette-Smoking Man stared expressionlessly at the screen. "It's Mulder. He's got the vaccine."

Without another word he turned and hurried for the door. Around him men were running as they began evacuating the ice station. The Cigarette-Smoking Man ignored them and headed for his tractor. There he was met by a gaunt man whose close-cropped hair was almost hidden beneath his parka hood: the man who had shot Mulder. He flung open the door of the tractor and clambered inside.

"What's happened?" he yelled.

The Cigarette-Smoking Man swung into the cab alongside him. "It's all going to hell."

The snow tractor began to pull away. Behind them steam vents erupted on the surface. Beneath the ice station, hot air blasting from the ducts was causing the ice shelf to melt and collapse.

"What about Mulder?" the other man shouted.

The Cigarette-Smoking Man glanced behind them and shook his head. "He'll never make it."

The tractor began to pull away. Behind them, mist rose like smoke from the domed structures.

Hundreds of feet below, the narrow passages of the buried spaceship filled with foggy condensation. Mulder swung his flashlight before him, trying vainly to pierce the mist with its feeble beam. In his arms was Scully, her limp body poised awkwardly in a fireman's carry. She wore Mulder's snow parka and nylon outer pants, and her face grazed his shoulder as she tried to lift her head to speak.

"We've got to keep moving," Mulder said hoarsely. He was laboring to get her up the interior of the steep, curving spoke that traversed the dome's center. All around them rivulets of water streamed from the hanging cryopods, pouring down to form pools and rushing brooklets on the circular central floor. The entire structure vibrated as Mulder struggled on, fighting his own flagging energy as he half-carried, half-pulled Scully as quickly as he could down the fog-shrouded corridor.

Approaching the place where Mulder first slipped down into the passage, the walls were now slick with running water. When they reached the end of the passage, they found the base of a tube and began to climb. At the top, they found themselves in the upper corridor where Mulder had first seen the prehistoric man.

Its body was no longer encased in solid ice. Through

the layers of ice and translucent skin the embryonic creature inside could be glimpsed, turning very slightly as
though coming awake. Mulder gazed at it transfixed,
then quickly turned and stared up at the ceiling.

"Scully, reach up and grab that vent."

She did not respond. He looked downward and saw that
she had lost consciousness. With gentle urgency he laid her
on the floor. "Scully, come on, Scully—"

He hastened to unzip her jacket, his fingers moving
across her neck as he sought a pulse. "Scully—"

She strained harder to breathe as he thrust his fingers
into her mouth, clearing her passageway. "Breathe, Scully."
He straddled her, palms flat against her chest as he pumped
hard, forcing air into her.

One. Two. Three.

He leaned down and put his mouth against hers, feeling
how cold her lips were, and her cheeks. He breathed into
her, turning his head away and listening for the telltale gur-
gle of air in her lungs.

Nothing.

He pumped her chest again, his movements growing
more and more frantic as her eyes bulged and her face darkened from scarlet to nearly purple.

One. Two. Three.

His mouth against hers, breathing; his ear against her
chest.

Still nothing.

Behind him, unseen, the embryonic creatures thrashed

within their hosts, as the ice around them began to fall in chunks to the floor. At the sound, Mulder turned and saw them striving to escape, and realized their urgency was even greater. With new haste Mulder continued CPR, oblivious to anything but Scully. Abruptly he drew back from her.

Then beneath him she suddenly moved. A shudder as she sucked in air, and then began to cough. The awful bruised color drained from her face, as did that dreadful panic. She gazed at Mulder, eyes focusing on his, and her lips parted.

"Mulder—" she said in a pained whisper. He lowered his face until it brushed hers, listening raptly. "Mulder—

"Had you big time."

The faintest grin flitted across his face. Before he could reply, a loud chunk echoed from behind him. Mulder whipped his head around.

"Holy shit—"

Through the haze of fog he could just barely make out dark forms moving in the corridor. Spindly arms and legs thrust from the cryopods, as their three-fingered hands beat and shattered the crumbling ice.

The creatures were beginning to hatch.

Mulder whirled to look the other way. The same scene greeted him: slush pouring from the pods as the creatures' powerful feet kicked holes in their icy tombs. He turned back to his partner.

"Scully! Reach up and grab that vent—"

Her mouth moved but no words came out. With all his remaining strength Mulder stooped and lifted her, turning to where the vent opened in the wall above them. He propped her against his shoulder and pushed her toward the vent. She grabbed it and pulled herself up, and then disappeared through the opening. Behind her Mulder jumped and found a handhold, propelling himself by kicking at what was below. With a hoarse cry a creature burst free from its cryopod. First one hand, then the other shot out, ripping through what remained of the host body. The jellied flesh slid to the floor in a gray heap as the creature grabbed at Mulder's foot. He kicked at it furiously as its claws slid down his legs. Just as it stumbled from its pod, Mulder yanked himself from its grip and in one smooth motion swung himself up and into the vent.

Inside Scully moved feebly.

"Scully!" he shouted. "Keep going!"

She made a guttural sound in reply, moaning softly, but moved ahead.

"Keep going, Scully—"

They inched onwards, Mulder pushing her when she no longer had to strength to continue. At last the vent opening loomed above them, a square of pearly gray light. Mulder pushed her through and followed, gasping at the bite of cold fresh air as he crawled forward. He looked back constantly to see if any of the creatures were following.

He and Scully were in the space formed by the air pocket, where Mulder had first fallen down from the ice shelf. All around them, the ice and snow which formed the walls of the cavern were melting.

Overhead a crater-sized hole had opened, and they could see bright blue sky through the whirling mist. Mulder shakily got to his feet. Again he looked back.

With an inhuman shriek, one of the creatures leaped from the vent opening, claws extending toward him. Before it could reach him, a blast a steam erupted and sent it hurling back down. There was a low, threatening rumble. More steam curled up from the vent. With a cry Mulder grabbed Scully by the shoulders. He threw her toward the far wall, leaping after her and covering his eyes.

Behind them, a volcanic blast of steam shot from the vent they had just left, exploding upwards and melting what remained of the snowy walls. There was a deafening hiss as the blast subsided. Mulder grabbed Scully and stumbled toward where there was now a sloping embankment, leading up to the surface of the ice sheet.

They reached the top; Scully coughing as she caught her breath, Mulder panting heavily. Together they staggered away from the vent. They came to a small rise and clambered up it, falling often in the soft snow. When they got to its summit, they turned to look back.

Below them was the ice sheet. A series of regularly spaced holes had appeared in it, and through these steam was blasting, defining the circular structure beneath. The white domed tents, dwarfed now by the gargantuan edifice under the surface. As they stared, steam from below blasted with hideous force, the sound so loud they covered their ears against it. Mulder grabbed Scully's sleeve and pulled her protectively towards him.

Through the cloud of condensing steam the ice station could just be glimpsed, like an abandoned toy village in all that waste. Suddenly the ice beneath it rippled, and without warning the entire sheet gave way. The ice station plunged downward, caving in to the very center of the buried ship. As it did so shock waves radiated outwards. The ground trembled as the horrified Mulder realized what was happening.

"We've got to run!"

He dragged her after him, the two of them looking back to see where the ice shelf was collapsing. Magnificent geysers shot hundreds of feet into the air, powered by the superheated core below. Ice sheared off in an ever-expanding circle, and steam vents erupted everywhere now; they now fled through a hellish landscape of smoke and flying snow, chunks of ice and burning debris. In the center of the collapsing shelf a black shape appeared, resolving itself into a dome as the ice and steam burned off. The black dome grew more and more immense as they ran, struggling to outrace it.

With a cry Scully fell, arms flailing at the soft snow. Mulder yanked her back to her feet, his ears numbed by the roar of the emerging spacecraft. He grabbed her hand, but before they could flee farther the ground beneath them sheared away.

They fell, and fell, and finally landed, hard, on the flat surface of the ship. As it lifted into the air they slid off it and down, plummeting through the air until they crashed onto the exposed ice sheet below. Ice chunks fell in a terrible rain all about them. Mulder crouched over Scully, trying to shield her from the deadly hail of debris, as the vast black hull of the spacecraft continued to rise above them, so huge that it blotted out the sky. Faster and faster it rose, gaining momentum as it broke free of the frozen weight of the icy crater that had imprisoned it. Scully moaned, her face pressed down into the snow. Above her, Mulder stared awestruck as the ship lifted clear of the earth, rotating slowly as it hovered in the sky. For the first time he could see it clearly, the network of spokes and cells that held it together and the smooth central dome.

It continued to rise, its shadow passing over the two tiny figures on the ice below. Mulder turned to watch it pass, the shadow moving like night across the snow, swallowing a small sturdy shape in the near distance—Mulder's snow tractor. And now the craft began to glow as with some unimaginable heat, transforming itself into pure energy. All around it the sky shimmered and pulsed, as the craft seemed to expand.

And then, with a last blinding, deafening burst of energy, it disappeared into a cloud formation. Echoes of its passage rumbled across the ruined landscape. The spacecraft was gone.

Mulder stared at the empty sky, then at Scully. As though

awakening from a fever dream, her eyes opened and she gazed back at him. Then, slowly as a child falling asleep, he lay his head down upon the snow. His body heaved with exhaustion; his eyes closed. Moments later he began to shiver, unconscious.

Next to him Scully lay, still as death. A freezing wind howled cross the waste, sending eddies of snow whirling down into the vast crater left by the ship's passing. Then Scully began to cough. She fought to lift her head, blinking.

She looked at Mulder. His face was white, his body limp. With all the strength she had, she pulled him close to her, cradling him against her body and warming him.

She gazed back over her shoulder, at the immense crater left by the ship, dwarfing the wasteland around them, two tiny figures invisible against the immensity and desolation of the endless ice.

CHAPTER

14

FBI OFFICE OF PROFESSIONAL REVIEW
J. EDGAR HOOVER BUILDING
WASHINGTON, D.C.

"—In light of the report I've got here in front of me—in light of the narrative I'm now hearing—" Assistant Director Jana Cassidy sat in the middle of the conference table, flanked by her colleagues. She held a slender sheaf of papers and glanced at them as she spoke, choosing her words carefully. At the end of the table sat Assistant Director Walter Skinner, his gaze flicking from Cassidy to the auburn-haired woman who sat at a smaller table in the center of the room, the chair beside her conspicuously empty.

"—my official report is incomplete, pending these new facts that I'm being asked to reconcile. Agent Scully—"

Dana Scully tilted her head. Her face bore signs of minor frostbite, but otherwise was healed. Her expression was even and composed, but as Cassidy spoke her blue eyes darkened with restrained defiance.

"—while there is direct evidence now that a federal agent may have been involved in the bombing, the other events you've laid down here seem too incredible on their own, and quite frankly, implausible in their connection."

Cassidy flipped through a file on the table before her. The faces of the other board members mirrored her own— curious and slightly annoyed. Only Walter Skinner looked uncomfortable as he shifted in his seat.

"What is it you find incredible?" Scully asked coolly.

Jana Cassidy suppressed a smile. "Well, where would you like me to start?"

As she spoke, a black-clad figure moved silently through the Dallas Field Office hundreds of miles away. Gray light filtered down through small windows set high above the floor, the only illumination until a flashlight beam suddenly pricked through the darkness. The beam swung back and forth, momentarily igniting jars, shattered plastic, twisted bits of wreckage. At last it settled on a table set up with microscope and magnifying glass, where several small vials were nestled in a cardboard box.

The man holding the flashlight moved quickly, silently, purposefully to the table. He was tall and gaunt-faced, his hair close-cropped. When he reached the table he extended one gloved hand and without hesitation picked up a vial, a tiny glass bottle containing fragments of petrified bone. The man glanced at the contents, then pocketed the evidence. As quickly and quietly as he had arrived, he disappeared, and the room was dark once more.

"—Antarctica is a long way from Dallas, Agent Scully," Jana Cassidy continued without a beat. "I can't very well submit a report to the Attorney General that alleges the links you've made here."

She picked up the file, then dropped in pointedly in front of her. "Bees and corn crops do not quite fall under the rubric of domestic terrorism."

Somewhere in the wilderness west of Dallas, a seemingly endless field of corn began to blaze as a phalanx of men wielding flamethrowers began to walk slowly and purposefully along the rows.

In the FBI Office of Professional Review, Scully shook her head, once. "No, they don't."

"Most of what I find in here is lacking a coherent picture of any organization with an attributable motive—"

Cassidy paused and stared directly at Scully—the first sympathetic look she'd given her since the proceedings had begun. "I realize the ordeal you've endured has clearly affected you—though the holes in your account leave this panel with little choice but to delete these references from our final report to the Justice Department—"

In an anonymous cul-de-sac, three unmarked tanker trucks sat beneath the blazing sun. A man in dark clothes, eyes masked by sunglasses, moved slowly alongside first one and then another of the trucks, painting bright green words and a gleaming ear of corn on the tanks: NATURE'S BEST CORN OIL.

•   •   •

"And until a time," Jana Cassidy finished smoothly, "when hard evidence becomes available that would give us cause to pursue such an investigation."

As Cassidy spoke, Scully's hand slipped into her coat pocket. When the Assistant Director grew silent, Scully stood and approached the conference table. She removed something from her pocket and placed it in front of Jana Cassidy.

"I don't believe that the FBI currently has an investigative unit qualified to pursue the evidence at hand," said Scully.

Jana Cassidy frowned and picked up what the agent had set there: a tiny glass vial containing a dead bumblebee. She studied it as, without asking permission, without another word, Agent Scully headed for the exit.

As the door closed behind her, Cassidy furrowed her brow and turned to Walter Skinner, her expression unreadable.

"Mr. Skinner?" she asked, and waited for his reply.

CONSTITUTION AVENUE
WASHINGTON, D.C.
NEAR FBI HEADQUARTERS

Fox Mulder sat on a park bench near the Mall, reading that morning's *Washington Post*. When he reached a small item in the national news his eyes widened.

FATAL HANTA VIRUS OUTBREAK
IN NORTHERN TEXAS
REPORTED CONTAINED

He looked up. A figure was approaching him. When it grew closer, he saw it was Scully.

He stood and handed her the newspaper. "There's a nice story on page twenty-seven. Somehow our names were left out."

Scully took the paper without looking at it. Mulder went on, "They're burying it, Scully. They're going to cover it all back up and no one will know."

In a state of great agitation, he spun on his heels and began to walk away. Scully followed him.

"You're wrong Mulder," she said. "I just told everything I know to OPR."

Mulder stopped and looked at her dubiously. "Everything you know?"

Scully nodded and they began to walk again. "What I experienced. The virus. How it's been spread by bees from pollen in transgenic corn crops—"

"And the flying saucer?" he broke in mockingly. "With the infected bodies and its little unscheduled departure from the polar ice cap?"

Scully looked at him grudgingly. "I admit I'm still less than clear on that. On what exactly I saw. And its purpose."

Mulder halted and turned to her. "It doesn't matter,

Scully," he said. "They're not going to believe you. Why would they? If it can't be programmed, catalogued, or easily referenced—"

"I wouldn't be so sure, Mulder," said Scully.

Mulder's anger had turned to intense impatience. "How many times have we been here? Right here. Grasping at the unbelievable truth? You're right to leave. You should get away from me. As far as you can."

"You asked me to stay," Scully said challengingly.

"I said you didn't owe me anything," countered Mulder. "Especially not your life. Go be a doctor, Scully."

Scully shook her head. "I will. But I'm not going any-where." Mulder's eyes narrowed as she went on, "This ill-ness, whatever it is, has a cure. You held it in your hand—"

She took his hand and gazed up at him "—if I quit now, they win."

They stood without speaking. In the distance, the Cigarette-Smoking Man sat in a nondescript car, his grim, dread stare focused on them. He took a last puff on his cigarette and flicked it onto the street. The car's electric window rolled up, and he drove off.

FOUM TATAOUINE, TUNISIA

Early morning heat shimmered above the rows of corn stretching endlessly towards the horizon. In the near distance, a man in traditional Arab garb led a second man in a dark suit through the green and golden stalks.

"Mister Strughold!" the Arab shouted. "Mister Strughold!"

Conrad Strughold emerged from the rows of corn. At sight of the man behind the Arab, Stughold's eyes narrowed very slightly.

"You look hot and miserable," said Strughold evenly. "Why have you traveled all this way?"

The Cigarette-Smoking Man stared at him coolly. "We have business to discuss."

"We have regular channels," said Strughold.

"This involves Mulder," said the Cigarette-Smoking Man.

Strughold winced almost imperceptibly. "Ah, that name! Again and again—"

"He's seen more than he should," said the Cigarette-Smoking Man.

Strughold made a dismissive gesture. "What has he seen? Of the whole, he has seen but pieces."

"He's determined now," insisted the Cigarette-Smoking Man. "Reinvested."

"He is but one man. One man alone cannot fight the future."

The Cigarette-Smoking Man held something out to Strughold. "Yesterday I received this—"

Strughold took it from his hand: a telegram. He read it, then stared at the horizon without actually seeing what was there. Then he dropped the telegram. In silence he turned and headed back towards the cornfield.

On the ground the telegram rustled slightly in the wind. The words showed stark black against yellow paper.

```
X-FILES RE-OPENED. STOP. PLEASE
ADVISE. STOP.
```

The wind rose, lifted the telegram and sent it spinning into the air. The telegram fluttered and swooped, rising higher and higher, until finally it disappeared into the sky. As far as the eye could see, row and rows of cornfields stretched. Acres of cornfields; miles. Extending across the Tunisian desert until they reached the horizon, where two immense white domes reared up against the horizon.

CHRIS CARTER is the writer and producer for *The X-Files* Feature Film, as well as the creator, executive producer, and frequent writer for the award-winning television series.

Mr. Carter has received an Emmy Award nomination, a Writer's Guild nomination, and two nominations for directing from the Directors Guild of America. He lives in Los Angeles.

ELIZABETH HAND is the Nebula and World Fantasy Award–winning author of *Glimmering*, *Waking the Moon*, and *Winterlong*. She lives in Maine.